To you

KILL THREE BIRDS

A KINGDOM OF AVES MYSTERY

NICOLE GIVENS KURTZ

KILL THREE BIRDS:
A KINGDOM OF AVES MYSTERY

Published by Mocha Memoirs Press, LLC

ISBN: 978-0-9840042-3-2

Credits:
Cover art: Maya Preisler
Editor: Melissa Gilbert
Proofreader: Rie Sheridan Rose
Map of Aves: Sarah Macklin

CREDITS:

Cover art: Maya Preisler
Editor: Melissa Gilbert
Proofreader: Rie Sheridan Rose
Map of Aves: Sarah Macklin

For Weston

PATRONS!

THANK YOU, PATRONS, FOR CONTINUING TO DONATE AND SUPPORT NICOLE'S CREATIVE EFFORTS AND WORKS.

- Aiesha Little
- Alledria Hurt
- Andrea Judy
- Bishop O'Connell
- Darrell Grizzle
- Joel McCrory
- Kenesha Williams
- Maya Preisler
- Paige L. Christie
- Patrick Dugan
- Rebekah Hamrick
- Rick Smathers
- Rie Sheridan Rose
- Samantha Dunaway Bryant

You can join these wonderful patrons and support Nicole's work via **Patreon**.

Go here (https://www.patreon.com/user?u=
19915635) to sign up.

ACKNOWLEDGMENTS

I would like to acknowledge the assistance and support of the following individuals.

Thank you to David Coe for his advice and feedback. Thank you to Maya Priesler and Trevor Curtis for their alpha reads of the manuscript.

Thank you to these amazing beta readers:

Susan Ragsdale
Andrea Judy
David Lascelles
Donald Kirby
Rie Sheridan Rose
Lucy Blue

OTHER NICOLE GIVENS KURTZ'S TITLES

Cybil Lewis SF Mystery Series

Silenced: A Cybil Lewis SF Mystery

Cozened: A Cybil Lewis SF Mystery

Replicated: A Cybil Lewis SF Mystery

Collected: A Cybil Lewis SF Collection

Minster Knights of Souls Space Opera Series

The Soul Cages: A Minister Knight of Souls Novel

Devourer: A Minister Knight of Souls Novel

Candidate Science Fiction Series

Zephyr Unfolding: A Candidate Novel

Weird Western Anthology

Sisters of the Wild Sage: A Weird Western Collection

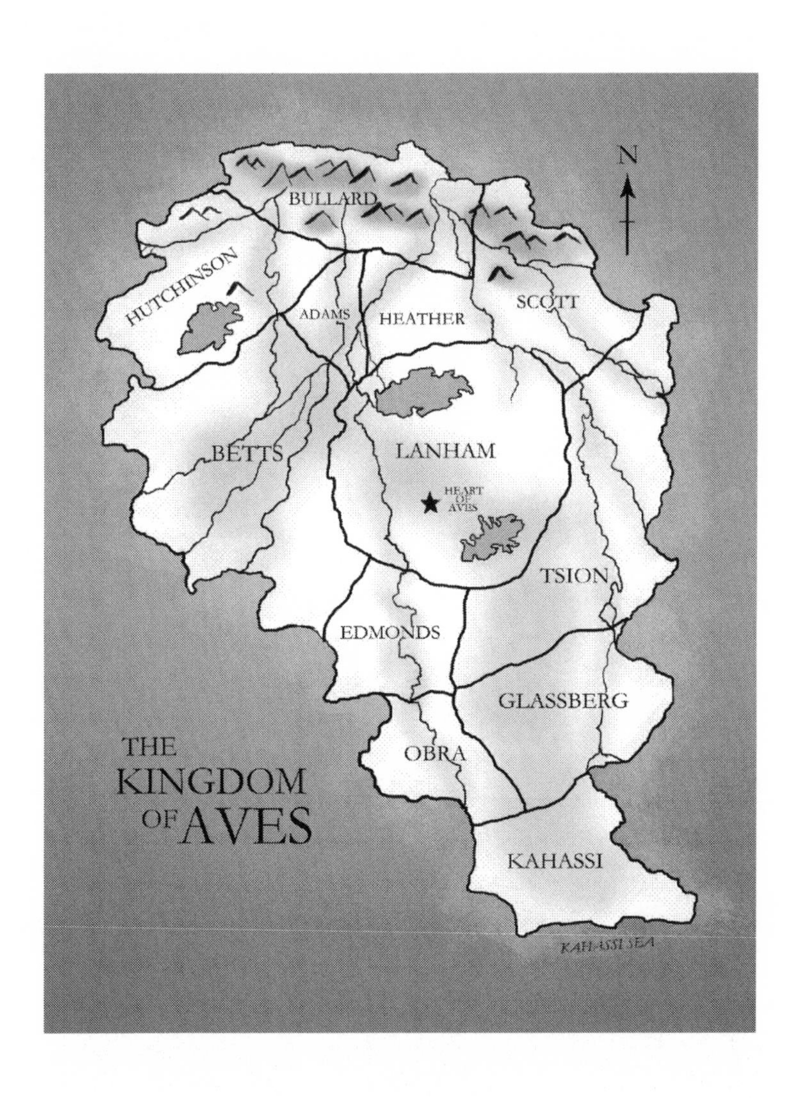
N
BULLARD
HUTCHINSON
ADAMS
HEATHER
SCOTT
BETTS
LANHAM
HEART
OF
AVES
TSION
EDMONDS
GLASSBERG
OBRA
KAHASSI
KAHASSI SEA
THE
KINGDOM
OF AVES

CHAPTER ONE

"You wanna see what a killer looks like? Look in the reflecting glass," Prentice Tasifa said over her shoulder. Her voice rose above the evening's insects chittering. Not getting a reply, she stood up and looked over to Dove Balthazar. "Anyone is capable of killing."

"Those who are with the goddess, and follow along her path, don't slaughter others," Dove Balthazar said, with a sweeping arm across the bloodied body between him and Prentice. The white, gold-trimmed sleeves of his cloak just missed the carnage. "Hawk Prentice, try to remember how this woman lived. Holy. Pure."

"She's a teenager."

Prentice pinched the bridge of her nose and sighed. Balthazar, like most in the rural egg, was about to discover the true nature of human beings.

Anyone was capable of great violence when dumped in the right situation. Doves like him only saw goodness in people. That was their role.

She put her attention back on the body. Despite the velvety darkness enveloping the site, Prentice used her skill to observe what most people missed. This wasn't a homicidal rage.

The body was covered in blood, but Prentice could tell she'd been hit with a blunt object. Her hands bore defensive wounds. A pit tightened in the bottom of the hawk's stomach.

"Do you want to talk about the skeletal remains found over there in the woods? We can wait on that one. Tomorrow will be soon enough." Prentice watched his face.

Balthazar paused, his index finger pointed at Prentice's chest. Her scarlet cloak, dark dress cinched at the waist and crossed with a leather gun belt that contained her talons, covered her entire body. The guns shot silver bullets infused with fairy dust for penetration. Boots and her utility belt completed her look.

"Skeletal remains?" He gaped.

"There's no rush. There's a depression in the grass. The trail has gone cold, anyway. Body's been there a while." Prentice shook her head. She stepped back from the current corpse, moving to the trail that snaked through the woods behind the church. Like most eggs, this one had a centralized location to worship. "The two men, suspects, who came here."

"Two men? How do you know they were men?" Balthazar followed her to the worn path, his white cloak grabbing leaves and other ground debris in his wake.

Prentice took out a cigarette, hand-rolled with tobacco. She snapped her fingers, sparking a small flame. She touched the cigarette's tip and inhaled deep and long. When she exhaled the stream of purple smoke through her nostrils, Balthazar scowled.

"Answer me, Hawk Tasifa." He coughed. "Can you stop smoking?"

"No," Prentice said.

"No, you can't stop or no, you can't answer me?" Balthazar's thick eyebrows rose in question. He removed his hat, decorated in white and gold. Doves wore them. "We requested, *I* requested, help from the Order. We have a real situation here. Some of my nesters are dead. The eagles have no idea what's going on."

Prentice sighed. "Yeah, and the Cardinal sent me, the hawk. Let me work. The smell of blood is disturbing and turns my stomach. I'm not a condor, okay?" She didn't want to explain to him that smoking kept her from puking at death scenes. Yet underneath the putrid odor, something else surfaced.

It hinted strongly of earth magic tinged with something black.

"How did you know about the skeletal remains? We searched the grounds after we found Gretchen…"

"Hawks see the unseen." Prentice pointed to her hazel eyes, wide and large, stretched from the bridge of her nose out toward her temples. From a young age, hawks' appearance unsettled others. She had spent a lot of her childhood in the nyumbani with her family. Her male siblings went out, to school, to work. Home-schooled by the rooks, Prentice and her sisters worked hard on their studies.

She adjusted her headscarf and sighed.

In her role, she saw what ordinary people missed. She'd been born with this gift. As a descendant of hawks, her mother worked for the Order. Trained as the investigative arm of the Order, hawks were dispatched to see what others could not. Now, here she stood, in the remote Gould Egg, a small community of three-to-five hundred people. A scenic gem situated on four thousand acres of sprawling woodland.

"We have a real problem here. Someone is using your woods as a dumping ground." Prentice rubbed her right temple. She dropped the cigarette and ground it out with the toe of her boot.

Balthazar threw up his hands. "Obviously. Who? You mentioned two men."

Prentice peered across the grassy swatch of land. Her eyes widened, growing and allowing in the unseen. Her wings broke free through the slits in her robe, lifting her from the ground. She'd done an aerial sweep before, but only a cursory look around. This time she meant to see everything. A significant amount of blood had been spilled on this U-shaped patch of land in the center of the woods behind the church. It splattered everywhere.

Prentice hated her abilities sometimes. There'd been no evidence to suggest there had been more killings, but Prentice could tell someone had been using this recreational section to dump bodies.

As she soared, she searched for disturbances in the soil or newly dug graves using her ability to see through the pitch-black night. She spied the heap of what looked like a burned corpse, the eviscerated body left in ashes. The hint of burnt flesh hit her nose making her gag. She spied tiny bits of bone and teeth buried in the ashes. Someone would've seen the blaze, and nothing around the body itself showed charring. It could've been dumped here and scattered, but who had the time? She could see Balthazar's confused and frustrated face as she flew over him. He wanted a fast answer and resolution. She didn't blame him. Killing frightened people.

When she landed beside him, she stumbled and grabbed his shoulder to steady herself.

"Sorry." She pushed herself to a standing position. Her stomach ached and her vision narrowed, growing more limited until all she could make out were shadows.

Damn it.

"Are you all right?" Balthazar touched her shoulder. "We need to get you back to the church."

Prentice nodded. "Yes. We can speak more there."

She made out that Balthazar had nodded and gestured to the carriage driver. The dove started for the carriage, and she followed, her hands out in front of her to keep her from walking into him or anything else.

"Here, let me help." Balthazar took her hands in his, and helped her climb into the back of the carriage.

Once inside, she ran her hands over the hard leather seats. The door's creak and then clattering told her it had been secured. Balthazar's girth rocked the carriage back a bit. In minutes, they lunged awkwardly forward through the woods along the worn path.

His quiet presence loomed in the small carriage. She could almost feel his questions. Indeed, she got them every time the Order dispatched her to another egg. The doves all had the same nosy inquiries.

"It's stuffy in here," Balthazar said at last.

Prentice heard the creaking of the window as he rolled it down.

"One of my abilities is to be able to see the unseen…"

"Yes, that is what makes your kind so invaluable to the Order."

"…but what many do *not* know, is that using the ability costs me some of my own natural sight."

"What do you mean?" Concern crept into Balthazar's tone, coupled with surprise.

"Each time I use my abilities, I am limiting my own sight. Eventually, I will be blind."

He gasped. "By the goddess! Is it so for every hawk?"

"It is." Prentice thought of her mother, very much alive in her later years, except she could no longer see. The Order retired her forthwith, and she spent the rest of her days in the cottage with her family. She could no longer see with her eyes, but her other senses more than made up for it. For her mother, her hearing became excellent and she worked at the church as an organist. She had a great ear.

"Sacrifice is in the blood." Prentice muttered her mother's favorite saying. It was true for all daughters of hawks.

The sacrifice ran in the blood.

CHAPTER TWO

By the time they reached the church, Hawk Prentice's vision had returned to normal. She tried not to use her abilities too often, for the longer she resisted, the longer she'd retain her own sight. Panicked shouting greeted the carriage as it rolled into the entranceway in front of the steepled building.

She stepped out to a gathering of furious church members, nesters, who bore lit torches and angry faces. She also spied a few axes and random raised goddess bibles Many people in these backwater eggs had never seen a hawk. Rumors and legends led their expectations, so she wanted to shield herself from those often-inaccurate beliefs.

"Just when I was starting to feel grounded here," she said to herself. She'd been dispatched here to make calm out of chaos, and so far she'd succeeded in doing the opposite.

Balthazar ignored her as he climbed out of the carriage. He put on his hat and he addressed the crowd, a glowing white figure amongst the nesters' dark browns, grays, and blacks. He raised his hands to quiet them.

"Calm yourselves."

The Order taught hawks little magic tricks to help them in their field work. She could conjure fire. The other trick was *fading*. Prentice pondered whether she wanted to spend her life-force on that trick. It took energy. It took blood. It helped her fade, or hide, from the average human being. She wouldn't be invisible, but she wouldn't be *visible* either.

Sacrifice was in the blood, but for hawks, so was magic. Blood magic passed down, which also gave them their hawk abilities.

The shouting became sentences that caught her attention.

"Do we need to be afraid here, Dove?" yelled a man from the rear of the throng.

"My son's been missing for weeks!"

"The east winds always bring trouble!" another person shouted.

Balthazar kept his hands raised. "Indeed. The Order has sent a hawk, but it will take her time to complete her work and reestablish our egg as safe. Go home. Be with your families and pray."

His soft, reassuring tone worked like a salve. Rumblings remained, but the mob slowly dispersed. Balthazar remained standing with her as they vacated the courtyard. Once sure they'd all left, the dove turned to the carriage driver.

"Thank you. You may return home to your own family, James," he said.

"Thank you, Dove." James inclined his head.

As he did so, Prentice realized the hulking man was a vulture. The sharp, black eyes and bright scarlet mark across the beak of his nose and mouth were common traits. Grayish skin stretched tight across the body and face hinted at a steady diet lacking vegetables.

"Surprised?" Balthazar laughed at the expression on Prentice's face.

"No. I mean, I knew vultures work with the churches for the graveyard work…"

"And other things. Come. Follow me. All are loved by the goddess."

"Hoot, even those who do not believe," Prentice said, almost out of habit.

"Hoot, even those who do not believe," he repeated, and gestured for her to follow him into the church.

They entered through the side door that fed into the office. The dove's upstairs living quarters had a guest room across the hall. The bulk of the church belonged to the worship arena, the fellowship hall, and to closets, storage, and community get-togethers. Like most eggs, Gould was the hub of its community. It sat at the foothills of the Adams Mountains in the Adams Nest. Like a sprinkle of confetti along its base, tiny eggs —like Gould—dotted the mountain range's base. All the nesters congregated at churches, and the entire egg depended on the church to govern and keep the peace.

He removed his hat once more, placing it carefully on the edge of his wooden desk. He also stood and removed his cloak, hanging it on a coatrack behind his desk. Balthazar wore ivory long-sleeved shirt and matching slacks beneath his ceremonial cloak.

Balthazar got the fire in the office fireplace going, set a kettle on for tea, and took out two mugs from one of the cabinets before sitting down behind his desk. He sighed.

"The thing about early spring. Warm days. Cool nights," he said.

Prentice nodded.

"I apologize for earlier. The entire egg is on edge. We've all been a bit high-strung."

He sat back down again. "None of this makes any sense. The Eagles came as soon as they could get here. They did a grid search of the woods. They didn't come up with anything, especially not skeletal remains. Their investigation tapered off to nothing. That's why I contacted the Order."

Prentice nodded. She sat in one of the two high back chairs facing him.

"The eagles have good vision, but not like hawks. It isn't their fault they missed it. In the morning, I can go with the vulture to show them where the remains are. There's another body—well, ashes, really, farther back on the green."

She didn't want to tell him about the blood splatter on the trees, the trunks, and the leaves. The eagles didn't look very hard, if she had to guess, or it blended in so well, even eagles' eyes missed it.

He gaped. "No! Such brazen attacks!" He mopped his face.

"Yes. You have at least three incidents of killing," Prentice explained.

Balthazar rubbed his chin in disbelief. "How? We don't have two people missing."

"Could they be crows or ravens?"

He tilted his head. "Maybe. They don't all participate in the official annual egg counts."

Not everyone who lived in an egg agreed with the Order or followed the goddess's practices. Some stood outside, in the outer shell—the outskirts—and off the Order's logbooks.

"We can investigate that more tomorrow, during the light. This isn't a coincidence, Dove. It's a pattern."

He tented his hands and stared across to her.

"Hawk Prentice, what can you tell me about what you found tonight?"

"It's early days yet, but what I can tell you is this: The killer is hunting people in your egg. They have troubled souls."

"What do you mean?

"Your victim had deep abrasions on the soles of her feet."

"Why?"

"The most important part of the ritual is conjuring fear and torment. You have another body that's been burned. I'm sure that person was alive when it happened. The other body on your land is in skeletal form. Once I'm able to examine it, I bet I'll find indications of torture."

"Who would do such heinous acts? It flies in the goddess's face. None of our flock would do this." He kept shaking his head as if his mind couldn't accept it.

"That's what I'm here to find out." Prentice didn't like where any of this headed. It meant long days and sleepless nights. "Have any of your nesters courted trouble?"

The kettle's whistle made them both jump. Laughing, Balthazar got up to fill their teacups with hot water. As he poured, he said, "I'm afraid I don't have any sugar or milk this time of night. My assistant, Martin, has retired."

"I usually drink sweet milk, anyway. What can

you tell me about the dead woman?" Prentice took out her pad and pencil from the pouch along her belt. As she did so, she bumped one of her talons, and it glowed red at the touch of her hand.

"Oh!" Balthazar stood transfixed.

"My talons." Prentice touched it again to get it to power down. She glanced up at the dove and asked again, "The deceased. How well did you know her?"

"Ah, yes, Gretchen Finch, the granddaughter of Geraldine Finch. They're the oldest family here. Almost half of the church is comprised of Finches. But Gretchen struggled to adopt the goddess's teachings."

"How so?"

"She was mischievous. She missed services frequently and hung around with a few crows and other scavengers."

"Any one crow in particular?" Prentice would have to talk to the crows anyway. The vultures, too, for that matter. She would ask the eagles to help, but she didn't know the status of those relationships. In some eggs, the eagles treated everyone the same. In others, crows, vultures, and ravens received poor eagle treatment. "You know the reason she's so friendly with them?"

The dove shrugged. "Rebellious, if I had to guess. Pushing back against the many expectations of being a Finch. I've seen it happen with some of the others, but never to the degree that it cost them their lives."

"So, not so holy and pure."

"Of heart, yes."

"I understand." Prentice made polite noises. "Do you have a name for the crow who Gretchen hung out with?"

Balthazar sipped his tea and clicked his fingers in thought. "I don't want to drop them in it."

"Too late for that. You have three people dead." She couldn't believe he would hesitate, considering the vicious attacks.

"Her name is Carlita Starbuck. The Starbucks live about fifteen miles north of the church. I can get James to take you out there tomorrow. Remember, Gretchen had a magnetic personality."

"That will be good." Prentice rose. She put her notes and pencil into her pouch. She glanced up at the dove's handsome face, pinched in worry. "It looks bleak, now, as do many things in the darkness. The investigation just started. We'll get to the bottom of this."

Balthazar stood and extended his hand. "Thank you."

"I'll turn in now, Dove. Thank you for the tea."

"You're welcome, but you've hardly touched it."

She took the winding stairs to the second floor where earlier the dove's assistant had shown her the guest room. The dove had given her the room across from his bedroom. Once she cleared the threshold into her room, she felt the stress roll of her back. Thankful to be able to let her dreadlocked hair free, she shook it and began removing her gunbelt, her talons, the utility belt and finally the large robe. Those remained close to her hands.

Carefully, she pulled her wings through the slits and stretched, allowing the cloak to fall to the floor. She picked it up and hung it on a peg along the wall beside her bed.

Outside the wind whistled. The pounding of her heart's beat slowed as she acquainted herself with her surroundings. It was a far cry from the glories of Landam and the smoke and mirrors at court. A throw rug bearing the Order's crest lay before the fire crackling with an orange glow, producing heat to chase away the early evening chill. Two towels sat folded on the room's sole chair along with a smaller washcloth. A round bar of soap topped the pile.

Candles flickered, casting shadows on the walls. She sat on the edge of the bed, pulled off her boots, and allowed them to collapse to the floor. With her remaining strength, she fell back into the pillows with her wings extended, placing them flat against the softness.

It had been a long day, and tomorrow promised more of the same.

CHAPTER THREE

The early morning sunlight didn't drive away the shadows huddled along the path back to the green and its surrounding forest. The woods had been cleared back a significant amount to provide places for picnics, sports, and the overall enjoyment of nature. Prentice fingered the heavy, but smashed, lock of the church green's gate.

"It's been forced." She turned her attention to James and another, nearly identical in size, male beside him. "Someone broke in here. Was it like this when you arrived to remove the body?"

James lifted and lowered one shoulder. The other man had the familiar splash of scarlet across his pale face that hinted he, too, was a vulture. "We came early, in the dark. I don't remember unlocking the gate."

She pushed on, taking in the scene in the brightness of day. Few clues appeared in the leftover debris of dried blood on vegetation. Whatever they had used to hit Gretchen over the head and torture her, they had taken with them. Something sinister had happened, and it had set the community on edge.

"They were organized and ready. This wasn't some heat-of-the-moment disagreement or slaying." Prentice crossed her arms. The body had been found not too much farther into the green.

"There's hardly anything here to see." Balthazar wore his Dove ceremonial robe and headgear.

"All right. Let's go visit some crows." Prentice adjusted her hood.

She followed James to the carriage parked just outside the entranceway with Balthazar behind them.

"This is where I leave you. I have duties with some of my members," Balthazar said.

Prentice took the dove in, studying his behavior and body language for unspoken clues. It didn't bother her that he declined to come along. She worked better alone, but something about the rush to leave the scene, when last night he presented such a concern, made her wings prickle.

"See you for now." She tucked that suspicion aside.

"I look forward to your report." He shot her a small smile before heading down the walkway toward the church.

"This way," James said, drawing her attention to the carriage. He held the door open and had lowered the two steps.

"Sure hope the weather breaks soon."

Prentice got into the carriage, and James secured the door. They pulled away from the church grounds and headed out to the egg's cobbled streets. The horse's *clop, clop* droned on as a natural accompaniment. Prentice spied the ruins of a wall that used to snake around the egg. They'd moved into the outer shell, a sprawling expanse. Everything crumbled, but then, on the other side, beauty. The lush and vibrant grass rolled over gentle hills and into the woods. They made their way around the river's bend and came upon a cluster of homes, sagging as if leaning upon each other for support. Wooden doors like hard trunks and rough roofs rounded out the common neighborhood features. Built into the forest, all treehouses, the homes blended into and made use of their surroundings. The smell of fish and other mixed aromas became more pronounced the closer they came.

James paused the carriage and called down to her. "Here."

Prentice waited until he climbed down and secured the steps. "Carlita Starbuck lives in the third one."

"Thank you." Prentice adjusted her holster. "You'll wait?"

James nodded, his eyes straight ahead.

Her palms itched for her talons, but she didn't want to go into a crow's house with them blazing. The conditions and contrast between the rest of the egg and this lush valley were like night and day. Nature grew in coordination with the residents, the sleek and glossy egg homes.

Prentice approached the door, and it wrenched open before she could knock.

"I'm Hawk Tasifa. I'm looking for Carlita." Prentice kept her hand near one of her talons.

"We're Carlita. We've been expecting you," said the person standing in the door's shadow.

Prentice made out long, black hair. Pale skin and dark clothing, decorated with shiny silver buttons and bangles, completed the outfit. They stepped out onto the narrow porch. Wide brown eyes met Prentice's. The home once had luster but had lost it over the years. Tree roots and branches threaded throughout the ceiling and walls. A massive tree trunk ran down the home's center. It contrasted with the linear wood utilized to craft the rest of the treehouse.

"You're a real hawk." They reached out to touch Prentice's hair.

Prentice moved her head slightly to avoid contact. "Yes, I am. Is there somewhere we can talk? Perhaps if I come inside."

"Oh. Yeah. Of course." Carlita retreated into the

house, allowing room for Prentice to enter before shutting the door after her. "We're sorry. We've never seen a real hawk before."

"Good," Prentice said, taking in the small, cluttered space. Fire in the fireplace, trinkets across the makeshift mantel. Shiny items everywhere, small and compact. "I won't take a lot of your time. I'm here about Gretchen Finch."

Carlita paused, suspended between picking up a throw pillow and sitting down on the rickety rocking chair. They recovered after a few moments, the smile returning and the friendly manner resumed. They sat down.

"Gretchen. Didn't think we'd hear that name again." Carlita hugged the pillow close.

"Why is that?"

"Well, let's see. We thought she'd fly away, on to greater things than our little egg."

"When she went missing..."

"Yeah. We thought the crazy bird was living the high life in some other Nest!" Carlita chuckled, but it was shrill.

"You haven't heard from her?"

"No."

They threw back their head and laughed. The humor made Carlita's voice light. It sounded strange at first, but Prentice liked it. Most of the crows she'd had contact with in her line of work had a cold as ice, unflinching, unemotional demeanor. Calculating and distant, crows didn't hold warm. She'd contributed it to a failure to connect to the goddess. They lacked empathy and emotional centers.

Not Carlita.

"Tell me more about that. The high life with whom?" Prentice remained standing and watched Carlita's face. "Could she have been abducted?"

As they sobered, they shook their head. "Dunno. Maybe something bright and shiny caught her eye. Or maybe she snared the wrong person's attention. Gretchen glowed like gold leaf in the sun."

"Did you ever see her with two men?" Prentice adjusted her habit to the stuffy room's heat. The little fireplace pushed out warmth like there was no tomorrow. "Anyone you know who wanted to hurt her?"

Carlita's cheeriness dimmed. Their shoulders slouched. "So, it was her they found over by the church?"

"You've heard?" Prentice cleared her throat.

Carlita closed their eyes and then rubbed their face in slow, sweeping circles. Through their hands, Prentice could make out muffled words.

"...We warned her...Rooster..."

Prentice perked up. "Roosters? What about roosters?"

Carlita paused and peeked through their fingers

at her. They swallowed hard. Reeling back, they sat up and glanced away from Prentice's hard glare.

"Anything, everything about Gretchen can help me find who hurt her."

"Yeah, we heard. Things have been different since she went missing. Things like that don't happen here, Hawk Tasifa." Carlita brushed their hands along their skirt.

"Have you ever seen Gretchen with two men?" Prentice asked, restarting the informal interview undaunted. She needed information and, as Gretchen's friend, Carlita would have knowledge of the victim's behaviors, secrets, interactions with others.

"Gretchen *liked* men. What she didn't like was her family. You didn't know her. She was strong-willed."

"Meaning?"

"Meaning, she did what she wanted. No one forced her to come down here and befriend the so-called social outcasts..."

"I'm not saying that..."

"You're being very careful not to." Carlita smirked at her. "Anyway, she would come down here, and we'd soar over to the various coops to blow off steam."

Roosters.

"Which coop?" Prentice paused. If she pushed too hard, Carlita would clam up.

Although grateful for the information, it added

an extra wrinkle to an already strange investigation. Coops tended to offer various feed and drink, a location that encouraged birds to frolic in all kinds of ungoddess-like behavior.

Carlita bit their lip. "It's dangerous. We've already said too much."

"Somebody dumped her like garbage. You haven't said anything I didn't already know," Prentice lied.

They shot out of the chair, stalked to the door, and wrenched it open. "Great. Then leave. Just go. You're a hawk. Figure it out."

"She was your friend. Someone killed her." Prentice took one last look around and stepped onto the porch. "You can help."

"Her death was like a knife to our heart."

The door shut softly behind her. Prentice spied James sitting on the carriage, staring off into the distance. *Vultures.* When she started for him, he roused and climbed down to get the steps and open the door.

Before she got in, she said, "Where are the coops in this egg?"

James rubbed his chin, his dark eyes narrowed in thought. "I tend to stay away from coops, Hawk Tasifa."

"But you know where they are."

He nodded.

"How many coops are there in Gould?"

"Legal ones?"

"They're all illegal according to the Order, but because they're outside the egg's shell…" Prentice shrugged.

"There are three that I know of, but do not frequent," James said in his deadpan expressionless voice. "They are down the road a bit, in Coopertino."

"Thank you." Prentice got into the carriage.

Soon the now familiar lunge of the horse-drawn carriage melded into the somewhat bumpy ride along the outer shell's roads. They traveled through the forest's maze of trails. Her mind turned to Gretchen Finch. While partying with two roosters, did she decide to leave? Did they peck her to death for trying to leave them without paying what they thought she owed? Did they dump her in the church's field to die?

It would be an outlandish scenario if it wasn't so common.

And why did Gretchen want to be outside the egg with the crows and roosters? She came from a church-loving family. Balthazar said Gretchen rebelled, but Carlita hit it closer to the mark. Gretchen didn't like her family. Why?

Prentice filed that away to ask the Finches later. For now, the rotting odor of death poured through the windows, making her gag. She fumbled with her pouch and pulled out a cigarette. She snapped her fingers for flame, and she lit the cigarette, smoking to dispel the horrid odor.

Are we passing a graveyard?

Outside, the lush calm of the countryside bled into downed tree limbs and fire-scarred land burnt black. Some structures stood stark against the blackened earth. Recent hollows and hovels dotted the landscape. Upbeat music wafted in, faint at first, but growing louder the closer they got to their destination. Ahead, the road narrowed so only one carriage could fit. If another one approached, someone would have to back up.

"I bet no one here could afford a horse, let alone a carriage," Prentice said to herself.

The carriage stopped, and James's clamor to get down announced their arrival.

"Where are we?" she asked once she cleared the steps.

"This is Dale's Chicken Coop. This is the busiest one." James gestured to the square single-story house about fifty feet away. Music poured out, along with laughter and a few joyful shrieks. Surrounded on all sides by dirt-packed land and wire, the coop looked like a place hawks avoided or else ended up on the menu.

Prentice blew out a stream of smoke. "What was that terrible smell on the way here?"

James stared at her for a few moments. Then,

"Oh! You said terrible smell. Forgive me. I was eating my lunch on the way over."

Prentice didn't want to ask what had died on his sandwich. Vultures' love of carrion was legendary. Them and Condors loved the stuff. *Blech.*

Prentice put her hands on her talons and started for the door. James didn't follow.

Good. She didn't need anyone in the way if things took a turn. Her talons warmed at her touch, and by the time she crossed the twenty feet to the door, they pulsated in green, ready.

She walked in and kept her head down.

"*Cacher*," she said, and bit her thumb, hissing at the pain, as she conjured the blood magic needed to *fade.*

With each step, she grew dimmer. The roaring music drowned out her footsteps on the wooden floor. Feed had been scattered all over the bar and the floor. Prentice found a spot in the corner, near the back, and watched. A waitress fluttered around the barstools and the few tables. At the bar, a well-built male in an undershirt and pants poured drinks. He had a striking plumage of long flowing red hair and a bright-colorful tattoo along his arm, which the sleeveless undershirt highlighted. His commanding movements and direction spotlighted him as the owner and namesake, Dale.

Everyone had facial and body scars, the results of pecking order fights. They decorated them with colorful ink and fancy embellishments like jewelry and precious stones.

How anyone heard themselves talk, let alone think, in this place. The constant shrieking and crowing in time to the music beat hurt her ears, but she couldn't leave until she saw what kind of folks gathered in here. There was a good chance Gretchen's killer was in this room.

"What can I do you for?" the waitress shouted to a patron at the table beside Prentice, tray in one hand, a cup in another. She slammed a drink onto the tiny table, sloshing most of its contents. "We got the usual."

"Whiskey. Feed special number four."

The pigtailed waitress nodded and headed off to the next table. Ahead, the bar rumbled as two men stumbled to their feet. It erupted into a pushing and shoving match. One swung at the other. A fight unfolded. Prentice watched the dominoes fall. One after the other swung and punched, kicked and screamed. Blood, biting, and a full-out brawl spiraled outward from the bar's epicenter.

Prentice didn't move. She wanted to see if (one) the whiskey would make it to the neighboring table, and (two) if the bartender/owner would do anything to break it up before someone died.

One of the reasons the Order discouraged fraternizing at coops is that chickens liked their pecking order.

It went against the goddess's teaching, and to be frank, it was violent and dangerous. It often came in partnership with alcohol, and the two things rendered deadly results.

Prentice sat in the back corner with both hands on her talons. Her fingers hovered above the triggers of each gun. *Ready. Always ready.*

A giant boom went off. The mob paused and then, almost as if thinking with one brain, they scattered through the front doors and out of the coop. The bartender stood atop the bar, holding a gun with his hair on end. Furious, his chest heaved. His stance with the weapon meant he intended to use it again—if necessary.

"Damn you, fowl idiots!" he roared after them. "It's just now noon!"

He stepped down from the bar, secured the weapon underneath the counter, and put both hands on the wooden structure. "Darlene! Clean this shit up!"

Darlene, the waitress, stood up from her protected position behind an overturned table. She nodded numbly at him, adjusted her shirt and shorts, and picked up her tray, before setting off to what must be the kitchen. In all, about four people remained in the coop.

"*Révéler*!" Prentice whispered, and the fading ended. She brightened, becoming visible to those around her, the few who remained, anyway.

Prentice made her way to the bar, picked up a toppled stool, and sat down.

"What will you have?" the bartender asked, not moving from his position and wet with sweat.

"Whiskey."

"Sure thing." He pushed off the bar and set about making her drink.

"Can you tell me if you've seen this girl?" Prentice removed a picture of Gretchen from her pouch. She held it up to the other patrons.

The bartender paused, turned with her glass in his hand, and shrugged meaty shoulders. "No."

"You didn't look."

"I don't need to, Hawk," he said. He approached her and put the whiskey down.

"I have witnesses who saw her come in here. She left with two men." Prentice met the bartender's gray eyes. He fidgeted. Most people didn't like looking Hawks in the eyes. They thought her ability to see the unseen didn't turn off. She did nothing to dispel those beliefs. "Where are those men?"

"Look, pay for your whiskey and go." He crossed his arms but looked away.

"I can get a condor down here..." She placed her talon on the bar's scarred surface. "Or I can use my talon to make you talk. You decide. I know she came here."

The remaining patrons quietly exited the bar, leaving only the bartender and Darlene.

"Put the talons away. Okay? A lot of people come through here. You saw that already." The bartender shrugged.

"This one didn't belong here." Prentice waved the picture in front of him.

He rolled his eyes and swore.

Darlene stumbled in from the kitchen with a wooden bucket in one hand and a mop in the other. When she spied Prentice's talons, she dropped the bucket. Water splashed all over her ankles and shoes.

"You're a Hawk," she stammered. "A real one."

Prentice put her attention back on the bartender. He paled. "The girl. The two cocks who left with her."

"Tell her, Dale!" Darlene shouted. "She's a fucking Hawk. They can kill you. They have permission from the Order to do that. I don't want them on our ass. We have enough to deal with those damn eagles."

Prentice loved how rumor and legend did her most of her job for her.

"Were they dating?" Prentice asked, putting Gretchen's picture away.

"Yeah. Been dating for months. They hung out here, away from her family's prying eyes," Dale said with a chuckle.

"What happened two nights ago?" Prentice sat back down on the stool but kept one of her talons out and in her fist.

"They got into a huge row. Right, Dale?" Darlene said as she came up to the bar.

He nodded. "She stormed outta here. Boris went right after her and Brian right after him." Dale shook his head. "They've flown the coop."

"Have you seen Boris or Brian since then?"

"No." Dale shook his head.

Prentice turned to Darlene.

"No, Hawk."

Prentice slipped the talon back into its holster around her waist and stood up. "If either of them comes here, let me know immediately."

Her lingering questions would have to wait.

She took out two bright yellow callers from her pouch and handed one to each of them. "Call me."

They nodded.

The doors to the coop burst open. Dale and Darlene jumped. Dale scrambled for his weapon. Darlene screamed.

"Hawk Tasifa!" James burst in with his fists raised.

"Yes?" Prentice walked to the door. She waved the others down. She stared up at James for a few seconds, shook her head, and started for the exit.

"Are you all right?" James asked, his face stoic but his tone revealing his confusion. He looked around the deserted coop. "I saw everyone rushing out, but you didn't so I…"

"…waited long enough to make sure I was dead."

Prentice cleared the door and started down the steps. She stopped at the bottom and turned to James, who seemed frozen to the spot—either shocked or appalled. "I'm joking. Come on."

"Yes, ma'am." James followed her to the parked carriage.

CHAPTER FOUR

As the carriage pulled into the front drive of the church, Balthazar approached. He wore a casual ivory short-sleeved, collared shirt and matching slacks. Outside the billowing folds of his ceremonial robes, the dove struck a handsome figure. Square jaw, warm brown eyes, and closely clipped woolly hair, Balthazar probably had more than a few fans in the congregation. Prentice smirked at the thought as she climbed out to meet him.

"I started to get concerned. Any longer and I would have called the eagles," he said, cocking his head to the side, but smiling.

James grunted something Prentice couldn't make out.

"I apologize, but I was following the evidence." Prentice turned to James with a dry throat. She cleared it. "He's a great help."

James nodded at the compliment but said nothing.

Balthazar chuckled. "Great. Thank you, James. Come in, Hawk Tasifa. I have lunch prepared and some sweet milk for you. I want to hear what you've found out."

Overhead, crisp blue sky and milky white clouds drifted along on gentle breezes. They walked down the open airway corridor toward the church kitchen. The dove strode by lush gardens; flowers bloomed in a variety of colors, and honeybees buzzed about in glee. They walked beneath connected arches carved from stone. They decorated the outdoor breezeway. Marble fountains in the goddess's likeness poured water into the cooling pools. Strategically placed benches provided places to sit and enjoy the splendor. Prentice spied a few of the church members among the vegetation enjoying the day's perfect weather.

The aroma of delicious food greeted her before they entered the dining hall. Balthazar opened the door for her, and she waited for him to enter. She didn't like people at her back, especially entering places she hadn't been before.

"After you, Dove."

"Hawk Tasifa," he said, gesturing for her to enter. "Please."

"No, after you."

The shift in her tone told him she would stand out here all day, but she wouldn't enter the hall before he did. If someone meant her harm, the dove would get it before she did. Harsh? Yes. She trusted her training.

"Come on." He entered ahead of her. She followed. A bustling erupted on the other side of the door. The entire church had turned out for lunch. Tables, complete with white tablecloths, were decorated at intervals with colorful flowers in vases. Voices and random laughter filled the space. Prentice paused just inside the dining hall and took in the view.

Balthazar turned back to her. "You don't trust me."

"I don't trust anyone. Don't take it personally."

He quirked an eyebrow. "You must have a lonely life."

They walked to one of the tables, already set for lunch.

"Welcome, Hawk Tasifa." A woman wiped her hands on a towel. "I hope you're hungry."

"Thank you." Prentice inclined her head as she took her seat. One of the hens, an apron around her round fluffy body, beamed at her. She wore her hair back in a bun and square glasses sat perched on her nose. She had rosy cheeks and thin lips. She smelled like onions and garlic.

"This is Martin's sister, Molly. They keep the church fed." Balthazar sat down across from Prentice. The servers were all men. Dressed in traditional

Gould male regalia—bright colored clothes and flamboyant hair filled with spikes and bows.

Once Molly had placed all the food on the table, Balthazar stood. At his standing, the others quieted down to silence. Chairs scraped the floors as others sat. He stood, and the congregation obeyed, instinctively knowing what to do.

Prentice searched the crowded room full of faces and wondered if a killer resided among them.

"Thank you for joining us today for lunch. This meal is in remembrance of Gretchen Finch. The Finch family needs us now more than ever. This time of fellowship and love for them will show them they're not alone in their grief. The goddess teaches us to be empathetic to those around us. Eat. Drink. And remember the love Gretchen showed us all, and to value the lives of your own loved ones. Tomorrow is not promised."

More than a few people sobbed. How anyone could eat at a time like this, Prentice didn't know, but Balthazar sat back down across from her. The clatter of forks on plates and glasses spoke to how wrong she'd been about that. Her belly rumbled in hunger.

"So, did you discover some good information?" Balthazar asked as he forked lettuce into his mouth. He chewed with his lips closed, unlike the person two seats over.

"I did retrace some of her steps and found out

some things. As I said last night, it is early days yet. There's much I don't know."

The dove nodded as he chewed. Once he swallowed, he said, "I don't intend to get into specifics here. We do have an appointment with Doctor Aiesha Little."

"Who is that?" Prentice forked her salad greens and ate.

Balthazar leaned closer to her and whispered, "It's a local raven who serves as the doctor...and coroner. James took the body to her for examination. She wants us to come down to discuss her findings. Tis rare for us to have such a death, Hawk Tasifa. We use what we have." He leaned back and continued eating. He shrugged. "They're quite knowledgeable."

"I meant no offense, Dove." Prentice picked up her glass of sweet milk. She would've preferred some meat with the greens, but beggars couldn't be too selective about what they received. The scattering of seeds among the lettuce provided texture and a salty treat with each bite.

True to his word, Balthazar engaged in small talk throughout the rest of lunch. He asked questions about being at the Order's court in Lanham. She told him about the grandeur of court and entertaining stories about life amongst the cardinals and falcons. Balthazar proved an amazing listener.

Toward the end of the meal, the dining hall had emptied except for several members tidying up the leftovers and dirty dishes. Prentice nursed her drink, and Balthazar sat with his legs crossed, sipping warm tea, comfortable and content. This was his element, and Prentice envied that a tiny bit. She had no such place to feel so connected, so free.

A man approached their table. He had blond hair and freckles. Prentice noted his wild eyes, sharp blue and restless. Her wings prickled and she straightened her posture. Her right hand went to one of her talons.

"Oh, hello there, Carno." Balthazar spoke softly to the man.

"Good day, Dove. I've come to meet the hawk." Carno turned to glare at Prentice. His teeth flashed in a quick, greasy smile.

A sense of dread fluttered down over her. Prentice met his stare.

"I am Hawk Prentice Tasifa." Prentice introduced herself. She didn't extend her hand for the right one rested on the talon and the left one held her mug. "You are?"

"This is Carno Finch, Gretchen's brother," Balthazar said. "I explained to your mother, that Hawk Tasifa is working. Later, perhaps tomorrow, she will meet with the family to update them on what she's found…"

Carno's emotionless face glared at Prentice.

Ah, you're the grieving brother. Yet it didn't feel that

way. Carno set off all sorts of alarms, but she didn't react. Not yet.

"It is nice to meet you, Carno, although I wish it were under better circumstances," Prentice said.

"Why are you here? Eating food when you should be searching for who killed my sister!" Carno growled at her, almost foaming at the mouth.

Prentice let out a slow breath. Carno had gone from a blank slate to full on rage in seconds. No, this wasn't grief. This was something more akin to performance or drugs. Whatever it was, it didn't reside in his concern for his sister. At this thought, Carlita's words came filtering to the forefront.

Gretchen liked men. She didn't like her family.

Before she could reply, Balthazar spoke. "The Hawk must eat. Rest. Same as you and your family. Now, leave us. We have other business to attend."

Carno didn't move. His hands balled into fists. His teeth clenched. He simply seethed. Prentice couldn't understand it. They found Gretchen's body yesterday morning. She arrived within mere hours of Balthazar's request.

Balthazar stood up and placed his teacup down. "Carno, heed my words."

"I want to know why she's still sitting on her arse!"

Balthazar smacked his hand to the back of Carno's head, and shouted, "Obey!"

The dove's voice reverberated throughout the hall. Prentice covered her ears. Carno stumbled forward into the table from the impact. Gracefully, Balthazar kept Carno from falling into the table completely, and steered him around to face him. He placed his palm on Carno's forehead, held his head, and began to pray.

Prentice slipped out of her seat with her hands on both talons. She waited for Carno's next steps. If he rejected the dove's prayers, she would blast him with her talons. The magic therein would restrain him and bind him. According to the Order, obedience to the dove's directions brooked no defiance. People had freewill, but—inside the church—the dove's words must be followed.

She had a feeling in her feathers about Carno, and she didn't like what it told her. Indistinct talking reached her ears.

Just then a shriek rose from the opposite end of the dining hall.

A group of well-dressed people, all pale and freckled, raced toward them. Prentice moved to stand beside the dove with her hands on her talons. The woman, taller than the male beside her, ground to a stop just before Balthazar.

"Don't punish him, Dove!" She had dull red hair and plain facial features.

Balthazar ignored her as he prayed.

The woman shifted her hazel eyes to Prentice.

"Forgive us, Hawk. We're grieving, and Carno hasn't taken our daughter's death well..."

The male beside her nodded in agreement. His hair, blond with golden streaks, shimmered. He also bore freckles across his face, but they added to his beauty. Although shorter than his wife, his dress spoke of careful consideration and meticulous decisions. Khaki dress slacks, shiny shoes, rainbow-colored vest, and golden striped shirt with a bronze jacket.

"Yes, what my wife says is true for all of us," he added.

"You're Gretchen's parents?" Prentice removed her hands from her talons.

"We are," the woman agreed. "I'm Bella Finch, and this is my husband, Oliver."

Beside Prentice, Balthazar declared, "You can stay there until you find your feet."

The dove released Carno, who slumped into the chair Prentice had vacated. Balthazar turned his attention to the parents and those gathered behind them. It looked like the whole Finch clan.

"Bel, Ollie, I know this is difficult, but the Hawk has her work to do. We cannot have these types of accusations and demands. She's working as fast as she can." Balthazar wiped his forehead with the back of his hand.

"Forgive him. This is a gut-wrenching time for

our family," Bella Finch said. Behind her, the others murmured in agreement. "Carno is anxious."

Balthazar studied their faces, moving his gaze from one to the other.

"I'm sorry for your loss. I assure you I am working as fast as I can to resolve this," Prentice interjected.

"Thank you." Bella cut her eyes to Carno. She started for the chair and collected her son. She hoisted him to his feet and threw one of his arms around her neck. "We'll see you again."

With that, she and the other Finch family members walked away, a human sea around their lone island, Carno.

She had a fluttering in her feathers about Carno Finch.

Once the Finches were out of earshot, Prentice turned to Balthazar. "What aren't you telling me?"

He stared after the Finches. "We have to go. Let's not be late to our appointment."

"What are you hiding?" Prentice asked again.

Balthazar looked at her at last. "Not here. Come. The carriage is waiting."

CHAPTER FIVE

As soon as the carriage door closed, Prentice said, "Sing, Dove."

Balthazar sighed, leaning back into the seat, and crossing his arms over his chest. "For years I've had grave concerns about Carno Finch. He's the oldest of Bella and Oliver's children, and the only male."

"What kind of concerns?" Prentice took out her pad and pencil.

Balthazar squirmed in his seat before answering. "He spent a lot of time pouring scorn over Gretchen. She, being the oldest daughter, sat high on a pedestal. He felt she should be a model for the others. At first, I thought his devotion to the goddess's teaching drove his concerns and actions, which Gretchen had rejected."

"And now?"

Balthazar shook his head. "I don't know."

Prentice left it alone. Family bonds could build up a person or destroy them completely. *Could* Carno beat his own sister to death?

. But *did* he?

She turned her attention to the landscape outside her window. This trip took them west.

They traveled near the Sugar River banks. In the surrounding wooded area, a rectangular cabin home appeared in the distance. Its chimney puffed out sweet-smelling smoke, and its rear greenhouse was fogged over. As the carriage approached, the front door opened and out walked a tall woman draped in black, but with a white apron. She put her hands in the apron's front pockets. A pipe was clasped between her lips.

"A Raven," Prentice noted.

"Yes. Despite living in the outer shell, she treats most of the egg's nesters," Balthazar said.

The tension went with them as they climbed out of the carriage. Balthazar greeted the woman. Now closer, Prentice made out the long braids tied back in one big plait and secured with a black ribbon. She had bright, wide gray eyes and a full mouth.

"I am Dr. Little, and you are three minutes late."

"My apologies. We had an incident at the church," Balthazar said gently. He bowed in greeting to her, and then indicated Prentice. "This is the hawk I spoke about on the call."

"Prentice Tasifa." Prentice bowed as Balthazar

had done. It felt strange, bowing to a raven, but each egg had their own customs. As the saying goes, when in Lanham, do as they do.

"Yes, well, come," Dr. Little remarked and went inside.

Prentice and Balthazar followed the woman through her living room and well-stocked study into a rear room where she saw patients. In this space, medical charts and 3-D models covered the shelves and walls. The consulting room contained an exam table, medical instruments, and other paraphernalia.

On one of the walls, Dr. Little had images of Gretchen Finch. Hand drawn, the images indicated damage done to her body. With a ruler, the doctor pointed to two chairs.

"Please. Sit."

They did as instructed.

"Dove Balthazar, you asked me to review the body of one Gretchen Finch. I have done so, and here are my results. I have released the body to the vultures for funeral arrangements and burial. You may want to touch base with the family."

Balthazar nodded.

"Let us begin. Gretchen Finch died as a result of a severe beating. The blunt object is consistent with a hammer or something similar. The first blow didn't kill her, but the next thirty or so strikes did." Dr. Little pointed to the picture where scarlet red Xs indicated where Gretchen had been struck. She spoke in a calm, matter-of-fact tone. In between words, she would puff her pipe.

"She was pummeled to death," Balthazar whispered.

"She fought back. She had defensive wounds on her hands," Prentice pointed out.

"Yes, she did. What you did not see, Hawk Tasifa, is this." Dr. Little held up a small broken nail in a glass jar. "I discovered it in her hair."

"Hers or the killer's?" Prentice asked. She ignored the raven's attempt to mock her abilities. In the rush of fresh blood and death, Prentice had overlooked the clue.

Dr. Little puffed. "Gretchen's nails were painted a bright purple. It is possible the assailant, during the course of striking her, lost a nail."

"Is there anything more you can tell us about her injuries?" Balthazar asked.

"Gretchen Finch was active, sexually, prior to her death."

"Rape?" Balthazar croaked. The idea horrified him. He became ashen beneath his usually warm brown skin.

Again, Dr. Little shook her head. "No, it did not appear so."

Prentice knew who Gretchen had been intimate with and, from the conversations with Dale and Darlene, knew she had been an active lover. But did Boris kill her?

She crossed her arms. The slaying *did* look personal. Someone clearly had hated Gretchen. The level of violence spoke to a connection to her. Strangers didn't devote this kind of time or energy to killing people.

Now that she had clarity on how Gretchen died, Prentice would look harder at Gretchen's family and friends. She'd already spoken to Carlita Starbuck, but she needed to find Boris and Brian. They'd been to the scene; their footprints put them there. She was sure they were theirs.

"We ravens have a saying. The blood does not rest until the killer is found," Dr. Little said around the pipe clutched in her teeth.

"Thank you for your time." Balthazar stood up and bowed.

"I shall send the bill to you," Dr. Little answered, one hand in her pocket, the other holding her pipe.

"Yes."

"It was nice to meet you." Prentice bowed as well and followed Balthazar out of the consulting room. She paused at the exam room door. "May I hold on to the fingernail?"

"I have no need for it." Dr. Little handed the glass bottle to Prentice.

"Thank you." Prentice placed it in one of her pouches. A clue.

She and Balthazar didn't speak until they were back inside the carriage.

"So?" Balthazar said.

"I want to speak to the Finch family. I also need to find Gretchen's lover, Boris, and his brother, Brian. Both are roosters."

"Roosters!" Balthazar rolled his eyes.

"Yes. Gretchen had an on-going relationship with a rooster named Boris. I need to find them and talk to them. Get the Eagles to search for them and bring them to the church. In the meantime, I want to talk to the Finches."

"I did schedule time with them for interviews tomorrow, but I can check to see if they're available today," Balthazar said, his face a mask. He leaned in closer to Prentice. "A rooster?"

"Why is that so difficult to believe, Dove?" Prentice peered at him.

His hesitation surprised her. Balthazar welcomed the assistance of a raven, but he couldn't believe one of his flock could be in love with a rooster, a group that resided in the outer shell.

"It isn't difficult to believe." He sat back and crossed his arms.

"But..."

Balthazar gazed out the window. "But, something Carno said months ago. He said he'd kill his sisters rather than see them lose salvation with the goddess."

"The goddess has no teachings about dating or being sexually active," Prentice remarked.

"That's just it. She doesn't. I counseled Carno on

his interpretation of the goddess's teachings, especially around love for all and peace. I tried to get him to see that the others, living in the outer shell, are still birds. We are one large flock. The kingdom of Aves thrives on its diversity. He refused, remaining staunch in his beliefs that those who don't follow the goddess's strict teachings were damned and unclean. Dirty birds, if you will. Foolishness, encouraged by his grandmother, if I am honest here. The Finches are a proud family."

"Gretchen's antics no doubt shamed them." Prentice recalled how fast the family had come to Carno's defense at lunch.

Balthazar shrugged. "At first, no more than any other Finch tossing off the reins to rebel..."

"But then..."

He squirmed. This line of questioning didn't sit well with the dove.

"Gretchen wouldn't heed her parents. Obedience is a pillar of the goddess's teaching, and Gretchen would have none of it. I tried to counsel her as well, but she would either avoid me, skip our meetings to go off to the crows, or simply sulk the entire time. She cackled during prayer and shrieked during choir."

He stopped abruptly as if he'd said too much.

"Why didn't you tell me this sooner?" Prentice pounded the seat with her fist.

"I told you she was rebellious. Her antics at

church had no bearing on her death." Balthazar looked back at her.

"That was for me to determine, Dove. It's entirely possible Carno killed his sister."

He agreed. "I understand that now."

From his reaction, she knew. Balthazar had suspected Carno, too. "Yes. Did Carno know about Boris courting his sister?"

"I have no idea. You'll have to ask him. He didn't tell me about any of that. I could never determine the source of his animus—except he detested her behavior and the effect he thought it would have on his younger sisters."

"You found none of this disturbing?" Prentice asked.

Balthazar swallowed hard. He seemed fragile. "It was no different than the antics of others her age. Over the years, there has always been one or two who buck against the yoke. We counsel them and let them blow off the steam until they return to the fold. They always return. I suspected Gretchen would be no different."

"Now you'll never get the chance to find out." Prentice plopped back in her seat.

The unspoken accusation hung in the air.

She glared at the dove across from her. Why hadn't he shared this information sooner? She could've been looking at the family a lot earlier in her investigation. Though, she had to admit, her training taught her to check with those closest to the victim and work her way out. She'd allowed herself to be caught up in suspicion of those in the outer shell, crows and roosters, thinking the worst of them, rather than adhering to her training.

"I'm sorry," Prentice said.

"No, no. I allowed my association with the Finches to blind me to how far some of them have wandered from the path," Balthazar said with a sigh. He rubbed his face, as if ridding it of disgust. His eyes lifted out to the distance.

"We all have our blockers." Prentice took out a cigarette.

CHAPTER SIX

By the time Prentice and Balthazar arrived at the church, the sun had dipped low on the horizon. So did the temperature. Early spring daylight brought much missed warmth and sunshine, but once it left, the chill from the elevation swept through, reminding all that here, cold dominated.

Prentice shuddered and hunched back into her cloak's folds. Lanham, the capital of Aves and home to the Order, lay farther south, closer to the hotter parts of the kingdom. Her home egg was located even farther south than Lanham. She didn't agree with these cooler temperatures.

Balthazar chuckled at her discomfort. "Once we get inside, I'll make you some tea. It will warm you."

Prentice nodded her agreement, and the two hurried toward the dove's office. Most of the church and its courtyards had been emptied. People went home for dinner. Lanterns had been lit throughout the grounds, casting shadows and light into the growing dark. A stark contrast to the boisterous but respectful gathering for earlier lunch, those same grounds that had bubbled with joy now lay in hushed quiet.

In the dove office, Balthazar busied himself with making tea. Prentice rubbed her hands together to chase away the chill. Her stomach grumbled about food, and she ignored it. She had more pressing matters. For starters, the broken fingernail that rattled in its glass jar. That had to come from the killer during their fight with Gretchen.

"Here we go," Balthazar said as he roused her from her musings.

She accepted the steaming mug and inhaled the aroma of lavender and chamomile. Hints of cinnamon hit her nose a few seconds later. Balthazar fanned the flames to encourage them.

"It's nippy tonight."

"It is," Prentice agreed.

"Would you like milk? I do have a little bit here."

"No, thank you."

"Come over here and sit. The desk is so formal."

Balthazar sat down in an overstuffed reading chair positioned on a Lanham-crafted rug in front of the stone fireplace. This tiny section of his office had been carved out as a miniature study. The chair, along with a matching partner, were positioned with two floor-to-ceiling bookcases behind them. A tiny table rested between the chairs where they faced the fire.

Prentice joined him in the study.

They sat in silence, watching the fire consume the logs. Balthazar sipped, his legs crossed, his eyes latched on to the dancing flames. Prentice wanted to talk to the Finches.

"I noticed you haven't touched your tea, again. I have something stronger, if that's more to your liking." Balthazar broke the quiet.

"I'm waiting for it to cool." She sat the teacup down on the table.

"I can see you are frustrated by something. Go ahead and ask your question."

"I want to meet with the Finches. Tonight."

"It's dinner time…"

He paused, seeing the expression on her face. "I will call them and see if they're open to you coming over."

"You could mention how Carno didn't want me sitting on my arse."

Balthazar groaned and stood up. He walked over to his desk, removed a caller, and blew into it. It squawked, and a bubble appeared, hovering in front of him. It filled with fog and squawked again. He put his hands on his hips and cast a weary glance at Prentice.

"Some birds are eating now," he said, more than a little bit irritated.

Prentice shrugged. "At least we can say we tried."

Just before Balthazar moved to cancel the call, Bella Finch's face appeared in the bubble.

"Hoot, Dove. Is everything okay?"

"Hoot, Bel. Yes, I apologize for the hour. Hawk Tasifa would like to come by tonight to talk to the family. If that's okay."

Bella Finch gaped at Balthazar. After several blinks, she managed, "What?"

Balthazar's mouth became a fine line.

Voices erupted behind her, and Bella turned away. From her position, Prentice couldn't quite make out the source of the commotion, but she heard Bella murmur hot, fast words.

"Sure. If the hawk needs to talk to us, and it cannot wait until tomorrow, we will receive her at seven."

Balthazar glanced at Prentice, before looking back to Bella. "That's fine. She will see you then."

He blew into the caller, and the bubble dissipated. Once he replaced the caller on his desk, he returned to his seat and picked up his teacup. A clock sat on one of the bookshelves. It gave the time as 6:12.

"Thank you. These things are never easy." Prentice stood up.

"They are *grieving*. Could it not wait until

tomorrow for you go interrogating them?" Balthazar snapped.

"The sooner I can bring a close to this investigation, the sooner they can process all that grief, instead of it lurking beneath the polished veneer of *coping*." Prentice left the office, leaving the dove to stew in his own anger.

She would untangle the twisted series of events that had befallen Gould. The other two deaths, possibly people who lived outside the egg in the outer shell, had flocks too. Someone missed them, but why hadn't those people come forward?

She shuddered and stopped once she reached the church's carriage lot. "Damn it. James has retired for the night."

The Finches lived in the egg. How hard could it be to find their home? She stretched her wings. She'd just have to fly over to them. The Finches would have the largest home in the neighborhood. If she knocked on the wrong door, someone would point her in the right direction. A close-knit community like Gould, everyone knew their neighbors.

Prentice adjusted her hood, securing it beneath her chin. She closed her eyes, and when they opened, she summoned her hawk vision. The landscape stretched, smearing until the joining of her human vision and hawk stabilized, and she could see all the perspectives—ahead, beside, and below. With a running start, she leapt into the air, flapping her wings, allowing her momentum to launch her body upward.

The cold made her wings stiff, but she forced them to work. Grunting against the goddess-forsaken chill, she huffed until she caught the wind and could soar a bit. Once she reached cruising elevation, she searched below for the Finches' home. Below, houses dotted the landscape, chimneys puffing out white pillows of smoke. The Sugar River cut a serene path through Gould. That river provided water for the drier areas of Aves. It didn't just stop in Gould. The Adams Mountains' ice-capped tops provided almost all the water for the Aves Kingdom via a series of rivers and tributaries.

Prentice's fingers tingled and had grown numb. She wished she'd brought a pair of gloves, but too late now. Her vindictiveness would be her folly. Her nana had told her as much. Could she have waited until tomorrow to speak with the Finches? Yes, she could've, but that wouldn't have proven the point.

It was part vindictiveness and part curiosity. A dangerous combination for a hawk. She wanted to push Carno's buttons, to get him off-kilter, just to see what he would do. It could backfire splendidly.

Just when she felt she'd flown to the farthest corner of the nest, she spied it. Glowing like a beacon on a lighthouse, the Finch house sat on the banks of the Sugar River, large and majestic.

Multiple chimneys and sweeping architecture that spoke to multiple generations of builders.

Prentice coasted until she landed with a small tumble about a block from the Finches' home. Everything vied for her visual attention. Crickets in the grass. Lanterns glowing along the street. The water dripping from roofs. She wanted to retract her hawk vision, but if she did it now, she'd be blind until her human sight returned.

She didn't know how long that would be.

Focus!

The wad of spit dangling from the branch of a rose bush held hints of blood. She could see the scarlet-bespeckled dots. Prentice pulled her attention back to the street that ended at the Finches grand estate. Ahead, the road narrowed until she arrived at the front gate. Wrought iron and heavy, it spoke to an earlier period of Gould history. It had a heavy lock and thick chains threaded through the bars. Fencing hugged the gate and sectioned off the Finches' land from their closest neighbors. These homes, dwarfed by the Finches, only had one story. Prentice wondered if these smaller homes had been servant quarters long ago and now held those descendants. Free from servitude, but still serving in the master's house.

Prentice spied the caller in a covered box position on a pedestal. She picked it up and blew. The scarlet caller shot out a small bubble, about the size of Prentice's hand.

A man appeared, but unlike the others, he looked like sour milk. "Finch residence."

"Prentice Tasifa to see Bella Finch." Prentice tried not to focus so hard on the tiny hairs along the man's nostrils. They crawled out as if attempting an escape. His hairline had receded, and his over-sized front teeth made closing his mouth difficult.

"Yes. You are expected." The bubble burst.

Prentice placed it back in the box and waited. She rubbed her stiff fingers and shook out her wings to pass the time. Someone would have to physically come down from the house and unlock the gate, and then they'd have to walk back up to the house, which —from what she spied—was roughly a half-mile up the drive.

Tall trees, evergreens, firs, and pines stood like sentinels along the sides of the house. The original architects and builders had cleared only the trees necessary to construct the home. The later generations had followed the same course as they expanded the residence. As a result, the trees now stood taller than the structure itself. A beautiful, lush forest existed around the Finch homestead.

A lantern bobbed in the dark as it exited the front of the house. Even from this distance, she spied one of Gretchen's sisters. Her cloak bore her initial, a scarlet R, and she climbed onto a horse. The beautiful sable brown mare with jet-black mane galloped down the path. The girl leaned into the ride as she went as fast as the horse could take her.

Prentice grinned. Still time for fun, even in the wake of one's sister's death.

The young girl reached the gate, climbed down and set about unlocking it with a rather big key. It took both her hands to turn it. Prentice ended up steadying the lock itself. The girl watched her as she removed the chains from the bars.

"Your eyes look funny. They're glowing. Orange." The child swallowed anxiously, as if she doubted she should've said it.

"I'm a hawk," Prentice explained. She could see the goosebumps and tiny hairs rising along the girl's arms as well. "Do not be afraid."

"I'm not scared," the child pushed out bravely. "You'll have to walk back. Muffin doesn't let anyone ride 'er but me."

"What's your name?" Prentice asked, seeing the cold sweat along her lip, even five feet away. The girl kept her distance, just out of arm's reach. Smart.

"Rachel Finch."

"It's nice to meet you, Rachel Finch."

"Head on back, so I can close the gate," Rachel said, gesturing with the chains for Prentice to move.

Prentice obeyed and started walking up the dirt path toward the Finches' front door. She heard the chains clang behind her as Rachel locked the gate. A few minutes later, Muffin and Rachel thundered by on their race back home.

The ache started in the back of her eyes, but Prentice ignored it. Too late to shut down her hawk vision, she swore at her own failed timing. Part of interrogating and questioning people involved seeing their reactions, their body language. She swallowed the throbbing ache, deep in the recesses of her eyes. She'd kept at it too long.

Damn her stubbornness.

She ran and leapt into the air, choosing instead to fly to the front door. She could have sailed over the gate too, but that would've been rude and an abuse of power. It would be the same as if she used her abilities to spy on Balthazar in the bath.

Prentice landed, noting Muffin and Rachel were nowhere to be seen. Fog rolled gently over the grounds, and the hushed quiet gave the area an eerie atmosphere. Through the haze, she found the door-knocker. As she raised her hand to knock, the door handle rattled, and the door yawned open.

The man who she'd seen on the bubble now stood before her. Short, squat, and serious, the man turned and started down the long foyer.

"Follow me."

Prentice closed the door and did as instructed. She had to force herself not to take in every single detail snaring her attention. She had to focus on the task at hand. The gleaming polish on the framed pictures, the candle wax dripped down the edges of the candelabras, all screamed for her notice. A sharp stabbing pain shot through her left eye. She grabbed it, hissing in pain.

"Madam?" the butler asked, over his shoulder.

"I'm fine. It's nothing. I've flown a long distance." She offered a grin.

He'd already turned around and resumed his pace to the great room. The foyer emptied into a semi-circular room with floor-to-ceiling windows that overlooked the Sugar River. In the center of the windows, a great marble fireplace and stone mantle stood. Above it, a portrait of a rather bland woman, round from wealth and privilege, glowered out at all who entered. All of the room's color scheme centered around gold and ivory. Three couches—arranged in a horseshoe—faced each other, with the central one facing the fire and the giant windows. A massive coffee table covered in a scattering of bowls filled with different seeds and grapes completed the center of the room. Along the edges were grander artworks and portraits of the Finch family matriarchs.

The Finches sat on couches. The *entire* family except Rachel.

"Welcome Hawk Tasifa." Bella Finch rose from one of the elegantly shaped sofas and came to greet her.

Prentice stopped. "Thank you for seeing me on such short notice."

"We knew we'd have to have this conversation eventually," Bella said. She smiled, but it stretched tight against her pale skin. Thin lips pulled over teeth.

"I won't take much of your time." Prentice swallowed against the searing agony in her left eye.

"Are you all right? Your eyes are...glowing." Bella fell back a step, her hand to her mouth.

"Yes. I'm fine." Prentice gestured to the family.

Rachel came in through a side door. She took off her riding cloak and boots in the alcove just inside the entranceway.

"You reek of horses," Geraldine said.

"Well, the barn is *right* there," Rachel retorted, her pink face pinched in annoyance.

"Go wash up," Oliver said gently to her.

Prentice came farther into the room and passed Rachel.

Heating this room during the long Gould winters must cost scores of birdsong, but Prentice didn't ask that question. Instead, she turned back to the family.

"Shall we begin?"

Prentice spied Carno's head among Bella's daughters. He wore a greasy smirk. Bella joined Oliver on the sofa adjacent to their children minus Rachel. Across from them sat four other Finches; the family resemblance stained their features. Prentice took out her pad and pencil.

"Let's do introductions. Tell me your name and

relationship to Gretchen." Prentice nodded at Bella, who sat beside her husband and two other individuals. She recognized them from lunch at the church, but she didn't know their names.

She wrote down their names as they went around. Bella's sister, Skylar, and Skylar's husband, Evan, sat wedged between the sofa arm and Oliver. Across from them, sat the family matriarch, Geraldine Finch, her husband, Robert Finch, and Skylar's children, two toddlers.

The clatter of Rachel's shoes on the wood floor interrupted Prentice. She waited until the young Finch got seated and comfortable before she continued.

"Tell us about you, Hawk Tasifa. That's a Kahassian name, isn't it? Judging by the markings on your face, you are what? Tisonian?" Geraldine Finch asked, her hands folded politely in her lap, despite the rude undercurrents.

The question took Prentice by surprise. Most people this far north hadn't even heard of Tison, and no one else had mentioned her markings.

"Yes, I'm Tisonian."

"Those three yellow dots along your forehead and the green and black ones down the nose, give it all away." Geraldine chuckled to herself.

As if Prentice was trying to hide it. She could explain the three tattoos across her forehead represented the goddess, her flock, and herself. The three tattoos along her nose represented the goddess's three pillars of love, peace, and obedience. Instead, she turned back to Bella.

"Tell me about Gretchen." Prentice glanced up at them. As she listened, she watched their fingers. She scanned for broken fingernails.

"At first, we thought someone had kidnapped her and was holding her captive. We couldn't grasp what happened," Bella said, swallowing hard and clutching her husband's hand. Manicured nails polished an off-white color. None broken.

"We thought someone had dragged her out of her carriage." Oliver brushed his bangs aside. Manicured nails clipped to respectable levels and polished with a clear polish.

Bella picked up the thread. "We scraped the earth looking for her, but nothing."

A circle of lanterns sat on the coffee table, casting a soft light on everyone.

"Tell me about *her*," Prentice explained. "Who was Gretchen Finch?"

"She was a bright star extinguished too early. She'd just started coming into her own." Geraldine Finch mopped her eyes with a handkerchief.

"She'll be in our hearts forever," Oliver added.

Both parents' hands, like her daughters, were clean and well done. Polished with polite, mute colors, just like the men. The broken nail didn't come from them, though it was possible they could've had them repaired.

The atmosphere was stifling. The massive hearth poured out heat.

"As you can imagine, this has been devastating to our family." Geraldine sounded sober, stern. "Gretchen liked to go to the crows and wallow around their shallow pools."

Beside her, her husband's face bore no expression or visual response. Prentice didn't know if the senior Finch could talk or move. He sat still, hushed and restrained.

"The crows?" Prentice asked, to be polite. She shifted her gaze to the siblings, the four of them all seated on the sofa in a perfect row, backs straight and hands folded in front of them.

"Yes, have you talked to them? They're shrewd and calculating," Geraldine Finch said with her nose high.

Before she could reply, Carno barked out a harsh laugh.

"It wasn't the blasted crows!" He pushed off the sofa, forcing his siblings on either side to complain and fall into each other. Rachel scowled. The other two daughters cried and held hands.

"Yes, it was! They'd do anything to get at us!" Geraldine shouted, twisting in her seat, back ramrod straight.

"Don't talk to your grandmother that way,

Carno," his mother interjected gently. Tears rolled down her cheeks. "Apologize. Now!"

"Gretchen was a cow! She had to be the bride at every wedding! The center of attention." Carno cackled, his wild eyes locked on Prentice.

"Carno!" His mother shouted, bolting to her feet. "Enough!"

"It's the truth!" Carno didn't break eye contact with Prentice. He glowered, his chest heaving in anger.

Prentice wouldn't look away, despite the growing agony in her eye. She could tell he enjoyed that they skated along the edge of an explosive argument.

"That's your warped truth," Oliver said in his calm voice. He frowned at his son.

Prentice watched Rachel, the youngest sibling, chew on her bottom lip. Carno's outbursts weren't new to this family, and it wasn't the effect of grief. The other daughter beside Rachel had her hands over both ears and both eyes closed. Prentice had been granted a peek behind the Finches' veil, and she knew she had to be cautious.

"That's right. That's *my* truth. You're all too blind to see who she really was!" Carno glowered at Prentice before stalking out of the room.

"My apologies, Hawk Tasifa." Bella watched her son storm off.

"No need. Outside of the crows, who else would

want Gretchen dead?" Prentice's left eye burned so badly it had started to weep.

She dropped her head and wiped it discreetly. She pretended to be making notes. Her right eye could see the right half of the room. The grandparents, the younger grandkids, and two of the five siblings as Carno had disappeared into the inner reaches of the house. The veil of normalcy slipped.

A thick silence took up residence in the rather grand room. It didn't feel quite so impressive. Prentice stood up, her movements slow. She'd viewed the hands of everyone. All well-maintained fingertips and hands that never done a hard day's work in their lives.

Except for one.

Carno.

"You can't think of anyone else who may have hurt her?" Prentice placed her pencil and pad into her pouch. She adjusted her hood. The optic pain progressed from throbbing to outright inflamed fury.

"The crows! Are you deaf?" Geraldine threw up her hands. She tsked and shook her head in disgust.

Bella came to Prentice and said quietly, "Our lives changed in that moment when Gretchen went missing and pivoted again when they found her dead. She was a beautiful, if rebellious, girl. She wasn't perfect, but she didn't deserve to die like this."

Oliver came up behind his wife and held her close to him.

"No, she didn't. I will find the person who hurt your daughter." Prentice started for the door. "I'll see myself out."

She made her way down the hallway. Thankfully, she recalled it led to the front door.

The butler closed and locked that door behind her.

Then everything in Prentice's vision snapped.

Oh, the irony.

CHAPTER SEVEN

Standing outside the door, Prentice remembered the half-mile long walk to the Finch gate and its lock. She stood under the lantern's beam of light. She could attempt to fly, but the idea of flying blind did not appeal to her. If she'd been familiar with the terrain, she would do it. She started walking, using her memory of her earlier flyover to navigate significant pitfalls.

The horse's gallop announced Rachel's arrival before she spoke. Prentice stopped.

"Hawk Tasifa, do you want to ride down to the gate?" Rachel asked.

"You said Muffin wouldn't allow anyone else to ride her."

"I can give her some nice oats to let you on."

"Then you'll have to walk."

"Yes, but I walk this path sometimes," Rachel said with a giggle.

Prentice shook her head. "You ride, but I would like to hold on to the saddle."

"Okay."

Prentice waited until Rachel took her hand and guided it to the saddle. They started down the path. She heard the nocturnal animals moving against the velvety night. The smell of the horse, Rachel's soft perfume, and the cold were all stronger than when she'd first arrived.

"Hawk Tasifa, you're not well, are you?" Rachel asked.

"I'm fine."

"No, you're not. Your eyes were doing funny things, and now they're closed and leaking."

Perceptive youngster.

Prentice remained silent. Hawks didn't broadcast their failings. She focused on trying to figure out what to do next.

She couldn't fly back to the church in this state. Perhaps she could sit by the Sugar River until her sight returned, then return to the church.

"Are you gonna find out who hurt my sister?" Rachel asked.

"Yes."

"What if it isn't the crows?" Hesitation made her voice shake.

Prentice kept walking along with Muffin and

Rachel. She waited. Experience taught her that people didn't like silence and would rush to fill it. So, she waited to see what else Rachel would tell her.

"I mean, it *is* probably the crows who hurt Gretchen. Anyway, Mom told her not to go around them, but she didn't obey. She liked to do whatever she wanted. Gretchen pushed the edge a little bit," Rachel explained.

"What if it isn't the crows?" Prentice turned the question around.

"I dunno. It could be someone else. The not knowing is hard to deal with." Rachel whispered this last. "Gretchen did some despicable things…"

"Oh? I'm sure she was just having a good time, trying to find herself." Prentice realized that Rachel parroted bits and pieces of Finch household exchanges.

"Yeah. She was fun. I miss her."

There. That was genuine emotion and original feeling.

Prentice heard the grief in those words. "I'm sorry for your loss."

Sniffles. Silence. Then a soft, "Thank you."

"Where does this forest go?" Prentice asked in an attempt to change the subject.

Rachel shrugged. "It's Finch woods. Uncle Evan said when he was little, he could sneak through them to bypass the front gate and see Aunt Skylar."

"Is that so?" Prentice found it surprising the residence had such a lapse in security.

"I dunno. The Reed family, that's Uncle Evan's flock, live over by the church. That's far."

Prentice nodded, but realized that, to a young child, the distance would appear great, but, to a smitten teenager, not so much. Was there a path that connected the woods between the Finch residence and the church green? If so, that could be how those bodies ended up there. She filed that tidbit of information away for later.

They walked the rest of the way in silence. The cold breezes brushed across them, stirring Prentice's desire for a warm fire and thick blankets. Her wings were stiff, but the fiery burning in her eyes had started to recede.

"We're at the gate." Rachel climbed down from Muffin.

The rattle of chains and the clatter of the lock announced the creaking gate's opening. The metal clanking disrupted the evening's quiet.

Prentice walked toward the gate, moving slowly and carefully, her hands on the bars to guide her. Soft hands grabbed her right one and tugged.

"This way." Rachel guided her through the gate and out onto the sidewalk. "Are you sure you're going to be okay? It's cold. It's dark."

Prentice said, "Yes, I will be fine."

She put more confidence into those words than

she felt, but the young Finch had more to worry about than a hawk's foolish pride. Prentice waited until Rachel re-locked the gate and Muffin's galloping hooves grew faint.

Once alone on the quiet street, Prentice started walking. She used her hearing as a guide, and remembered that most of the road ahead didn't have anything to run into per se. The gurgling Sugar River drew her attention and she drifted closer to the sound. She slowed and, feeling the bushes blocking her path, lowered herself to the ground. Here she'd wait until her sight returned and then head back to the church.

She placed both hands on her talons, lowered her head, and dozed.

PRENTICE'S EYES FLAPPED OPEN, and she bolted awake with both talons pointed in the direction of the noise. She could make out shadows—two, maybe three—hovering in front of her. From what she could gather, it was still night or early morning dark.

"Ma'am, I'm Eagle Jamison, and this is Eagle O'Neil. We got a call of a suspicious person loitering around the neighborhood," he said. "You'll want to put those weapons away and come with us before someone gets hurt."

They smelled like eagles, earthy and fishy. They

also sounded like eagles. Their arrogant tone held nothing but contempt for the subject they addressed. They often entertained the illusion that, as eagles, they were the order of the egg and them alone, a mistake that led to abuses of authority and loss of life. Prentice frowned at the intrusion.

Why are they here, bothering me?

Prentice pushed herself to stand, both talons pointed at the two shadowy figures. "I'm Hawk Tasifa. I'm not going anywhere. I'm not doing anything wrong or that violates the order here."

"A hawk?" The other eagle, O'Neil, barked out a laugh. "We don't need hawks up here."

"Look, clearly you don't belong in this neighborhood…" Eagle Jamison reached for her.

Prentice fired with limited visibility. The eagles' approach, by design, was meant to unsettle and disarm. It wasn't working.

The eagles scrambled, pulling out their own shields to protect themselves. She missed, but that had been the point. They didn't know she couldn't see a damn thing.

"Ma'am!" Eagle Jamison, angry, and more than a little scared, shouted. "This is a residential neighborhood. Put down your weapons."

"No. I'm Hawk Tasifa, requested by Dove Balthazar Rue to investigate the death of Gretchen Finch. I was just sitting here, minding my own business, when you two *pigeons* show up to harass me."

Prentice didn't like that some nosy neighbor, probably someone within the Finches' home, called the eagles on her. "So, go back to whomever called this in and tell them to stuff it. Or better, call the dove and ask him. I'll wait."

Damn her vision. She wished her eyes to repair themselves faster. They'd need to contact Balthazar and that would take time, which she needed.

Eagle Jamison sounded shaken up, but he said, "All right. I'll call the dove."

The shadows moved back. Prentice kept her guard and her talons up. She didn't actually trust them, but she could hear the caller's squawk and then see what could've been a cloudy bubble. Or at least that was what she thought she was seeing based on what she could make out.

After several minutes, one of the two eagles approached her, with his hands up.

"I apologize, Hawk Tasifa. Dove Balthazar asked us to return you to the church," Eagle Jamison said, his tone humbler than before. Balthazar must've have set them right.

Prentice didn't lower her talons. It could be a trap to get her into the carriage.

"Please, lower your talons."

Prentice remained in position. Although not in severe danger, she was at the eagles' mercy.

"He said you'd be resistant. So, he also said to tell you, he will have your sweet milk, whatever that is, when you arrive," Eagle Jamison said with relief. "I'm glad the dove confirmed your identity."

"Okay." Prentice lowered her talons and placed them in their holsters.

"Thank you! Now, if you'll follow me," Eagle Jamison said.

Prentice could make out figures carved from darkness and managed to get into the carriage along with Eagle Jamison. The other eagle had climbed up top to drive the carriage. With a shout, they pulled forward into the night. The lantern-lit streets soon faded away as they left the residential area. Prentice closed her eyes. In the carriage's dark interior, the eagle wouldn't be able to make out her face anyway.

After several minutes of hushed quiet, Eagle Jamison, broke it. "We don't get hawks up this way. I'm sorry we didn't believe you."

Prentice shrugged. "It's over now."

"I should've recognized your talons. No one has those but hawks," he added.

"Have you seen talons before?"

"Only in the training manuscripts."

"Then you wouldn't have been able to identify them. A hawk's talons are different for each individual person."

"Oh. I didn't know that. Tell me, we found Gretchen Finch, but there was something other about her death," he said. "That's why the dove called the Order. Would've been nice of him to tell us you'd arrived."

"Yes. What do you mean, *other*?" Prentice sat up straighter and shook off the desire to doze.

Eagle Jamison shifted in the seat across from her. "Clearly, someone beat her to death. With a blunt object, if I had to guess. But the body wasn't there the day before. We searched the entire church green. Nothing. In fact, we worked our way from the church outward to the woods."

"So when the body appeared on the green…"

"It must've been either one of two things. One, someone dumped her there, but they'd have to get by the eagle we'd placed to watch over the green and the lock on the gate. Or two, magic."

"The lock was forced. Still, what kind of magic?"

"Well, I dunno. I'm not a hawk." Eagle Jamison smirked. "But the body didn't smell right. It didn't seem right if you take my meaning."

"I do." Prentice pondered the eagle's information.

"It's so surreal."

"What is?"

"You being here. Gretchen being dead…" Eagle Jamison trailed off. "It's always hard when you know the victim."

"Who's in charge of the investigation?" Prentice asked, shifting the topic away from emotions and back to facts.

"We're only an office of ten. O'Neil and I are the senior members, but I am the head investigator," Jamison explained.

The carriage slowed to a trot and made several turns as it snaked through the streets to the church. She'd come into Gould this way and could tell from the scent of oak and pine trees, and something sweet, that they were close to the church.

"Did Gretchen have a lover?" Prentice asked.

Quiet. Then Eagle Jamison said with a heavy sigh, "You're gonna hear this anyway, but yeah. She courted Boris, a local rooster."

"Did you talk to Boris?"

"We can't find him. We sent out a team of four to search the outer shell for both Boris and his brother, Brian, but so far, no success. They might have flown to other parts."

"Maybe," Prentice said. From Darlene and Dale's account, Boris had loved Gretchen. He wouldn't leave if she was missing, and definitely not once she'd been found dead. He might hide from the eagles, but so did most in the outer shell.

"You don't believe it was him. Do you?" Eagle Jamison asked.

She could hear the smirk in his tone.

"I don't know. I would like to talk to him, so it's important we find him. Can you double your efforts?"

"Sure. Anything to help the Order," he said.

It didn't sound like he meant it.

It didn't matter. She'd hold him to it.

The carriage stopped.

"I'll come by later today to get more information about the investigation," she said. Her vision hadn't returned, but it had improved from shadows to more defined images and colorful blurs.

"Sure. I'm on the evening shift, but I'll leave directions for Eagle Kovacs."

She got out and waiting for her, with his arms folded in complete disapproval, stood Balthazar Rue. He wore an ivory robe and matching slippers.

"You just had to go over there tonight." Balthazar rubbed the bridge of his nose.

"It went well. It isn't my fault the neighborhood is a group of elites," Prentice said. She started up to her room.

"I placed some sweet milk beside your bed. We'll talk in the morning."

"Make it afternoon." Prentice waved good night and entered the church.

Balthazar followed, making sure to lock the doors. Prentice took the steps two at a time, despite her body singing in fatigue and agony. She was tired of dealing with people and their secrets. Now, she wanted to recharge and heal.

Balthazar disappeared down the stairwell again.

Once she got the guest room's door closed, she removed her belt, her holster, and her talons. Her body hurt. She took the sweet milk in hand and sat down in the center of the bed. While she sipped the soothing liquid, she removed her healing kit from one of the pouches on her utility belt. She'd delayed using it earlier because she couldn't see anything. She couldn't spend time wandering in the woods.

In the room's warmth, she removed the metal tin of shea butter balm. The pleasant scent reminded her of home, her *real* home, not the cold indifference of the Lanham court. Tison, the egg by the sea. The aroma called up warm sands and cool sea-salted breezes. Laughter and succulent mangoes or crunchy coconuts.

Using her thumb, she worked the lid off and dipped in her index finger to scoop out a tiny bit. She spread it across her upper cheeks and then around her eyes.

She whispered, "*Uponyaji*."

Bright cerulean sparks sprouted, and she closed her eyes. It stung. She spied the magic working through slits. It rushed to the spots, and it didn't cause any additional agony. The pain fed into the lingering pain she already suffered.

She panted as if she'd run a great distance as it warmed. Tomorrow, she'd have bruising around her eyes and upper cheeks, but nothing too horrible.

The smell of the shea butter brought back more memories of home. The local watering hole where all the birds gathered. Her parents and uncles, aunties and cousins all dressed in their traditional colors of vibrant greens and scarlet reds, royal purples and stunning blues. Her mother's hands, braiding her hair, and her little sister's laughter at the faces Prentice made. Despite her mother's blindness, she knew how to braid and lock the strands of her hair.

Prentice sighed. She missed her family. Since being dispatched to the Order's court at fourteen, she hadn't had a lot of time to return. Perhaps after this case, she'd be able to go home. A glimmer of hope rose in her heart.

She finished the milk and lay back on the bed, allowing the magic to continue to heal the optic nerves in her eyes and repair the damage to her hawk abilities.

Tomorrow, she would go back to the church green and look at the ashes and the skeletal remains, if Balthazar hadn't had them removed. She couldn't shake the fact that the three deaths had to be connected. Although Gretchen's killing had been the most prominent and the reason she'd been dispatched to Gould, the other two people most likely had families and friends too. Why hadn't they been reported missing?

Maybe they had been. If they lived outside the egg, Balthazar wouldn't have any reason to know, but the eagles would. They were responsible for the entire egg, including the outer shell.

With the following day mapped out, Prentice

shifted her thinking into meditation. She didn't want to deplete her life energy while healing.

Her wings stretched wide and then wrapped around her. She hummed a song her mother had taught her. The words didn't translate into the High Speech because it had been passed down before the hawks were members of the Order. When her people, and others like them, didn't belong to the kingdom. The kingdom didn't even *exist*.

Prentice pulled her wings closer, feeling their warmth and softness against her skin. She cleared her mind and continued to hum, moving into chanting the chorus. Her body lifted from the bed, buoyed by the internal magic housed in her core. Derived from the ancestral power of the women who came before, it pooled in her blood. She couldn't see it, her eyes were closed, but she had seen others in the cocoon, lifting her and placing their hands on her. In this, they sent their strength into her. It came with a beautiful cerulean glow.

The words filled the room as her ancestors joined in. Eventually, they too fell away. Nothing existed except Prentice in the warm embrace of the cocoon formed by her wings and her magic. It pulsated across her skin, across her feathers, and kept cadence with her heartbeat.

Prentice allowed the magic to envelope and heal her.

She still had work to do.

CHAPTER EIGHT

Golden rays poured sunlight onto the lush church green. Prentice stood at the spot where the pile of ashes remained. A secluded area shielded by trees with giant leaves, the pile of ashes didn't show any signs of a struggle on the vegetation around the blackened bits. The scene hit her as weird. Now, in the illumination of day, she took in more than she had a few days ago, when her attention had been focused on Gretchen's body.

Why burn it? Why not leave it for discovery like Gretchen?

The killer had been angry and wanted to punish the victim, inflicting as much pain as possible. But even more so, he wanted her erased. Gone. Obliterated.

Prentice had bad vibes about all of this. She crouched down and inhaled. Sure enough, beneath the char were hints of musty magic, the same earthy notes she had smelled around Gretchen's body. Same killer. She took her hand and carefully dug into the pile. Had the killer snapped and killed this person with flame? It had to have been conjured. Ordinary fire would've burned through all of the surrounding field, and it probably would've drawn the dove's attention.

A deafening silence descended over the spot. No animals prowling. No insects. A growing sense of emptiness settled inside her. She crouched down and dug her fingers through the ashes. There! Her fingers came in contact with hardened objects in the soft, flaky ash. Once she blew off the soot, she recognized them as bits of teeth and bone. She took out a small glass container and slipped them into it. She'd have to try to dowse them to see if she could discern the identity of the person.

As she stood, she sighed. She moved across the green to the other body, the skeletal remains. It looked pretty well intact. Her investigation progressed slowly, like paint fading. The stench of rotten flesh had disappeared long ago. Only hints remained, those tiny bits clinging to bones. She crouched down here as well, careful not to get too close and disturb something important. The remains had been here a while.

This person had been the first one to die. Strings of hair clung to the head. A grown individual if the skeletal length was any indication. The forearms bore cut marks on the bones. This killing would've been grisly, and—judging by the dried blood on the vegetation—it happened here.

How did the eagles miss this?

She searched the area around the remains. This far back on the green and so close to the woods, the attacker could have lain in wait. Judging by the pelvis, she noted this victim, too, was a woman. What precarious situation had landed her here?

Three women had all been slain and dumped. If she had to guess, by the same calloused and troubled soul. Was this a statement against the church?

Prentice leaned over and plucked the strands of hair from the head and placed them in another glass container. She needed to solve these women's murders before more happened.

She stood up.

"Hawk Tasifa!" shouted Balthazar from the path. He waved.

From this distance, he sounded drained. Prentice approached him with her newfound clues in her utility belt. Once she reached him, she asked, "Yes?"

"Have you eaten today? I haven't had a chance to read your letter. Morning meditation just ended." Balthazar was dressed in a long-sleeved ivory shirt and matching slacks. Clearly, he cleaned up after meditation. He looked as fresh as if he'd been washed and dried on the line. He wore polished dark brown boots.

"Yes." Prentice frowned at the fact he had called her over to ask that simple question. "Do you know any missing non-egg members?"

Balthazar huffed. "You've asked me that before, but I don't know of any."

"You've had a few days to think about it."

"I…I don't know of anyone." Balthazar sighed. "The eagles should know."

"I'm heading that way."

"Will you need use of the carriage?" Balthazar looked down the pathway to the gate where James and the dove's carriage already waited.

"Yes."

"I figured." Balthazar laughed. "Do keep me included in what you find. Yes?"

"Of course. Real quick, Dove. Who does earth magic around here?"

Balthazar paused. His index finger tapped his chin. "Most of the birds have access to varying degrees of earth magic, though we don't have any true mages. The truly gifted ones get recruited down to Lanham."

"Okay. Who are the strongest ones here?"

"Geraldine Finch is one of the oldest and strongest earth magic practitioners in the egg."

"Why doesn't that surprise me?"

"You keep focusing on that family. You're being really thorough."

"Because that's where the evidence keeps leading, Dove." Prentice threw up her hands.

"What evidence? I've not seen any."

"I see what is unseen, Dove. That's why you sent for a hawk. Now that I'm here, I'm going to do my job."

"Geraldine has already threatened to make a complaint to the Order about you, and include me." Balthazar held his ground.

"I'm going to follow this wherever it leads."

"I understand. I do, but I live here. I'll be here after you're gone."

"Why? Did you ask yourself why the grandmother of a slain victim would complain about a hawk doing her duties, which means asking questions?" Prentice glared at him. "There's something foul in that household, Dove, and I believe it got Gretchen killed."

Balthazar looked dazed, as if her words had been pebbles pummeling the glass views of his members.

"You believe that?"

She could hear the anguish in his voice.

"Yes. Anyone is capable of killing. More importantly, I'm going to prove it."

The knowledge Geraldine Finch had earth magic power could crack the case wide open.

Prentice stormed off toward the gate, leaving

Balthazar gaping after her. She didn't have time to debate the politics of egg life. She had three killings to solve.

"This way, Hawk Tasifa." James opened the carriage door, once Prentice cleared the gate.

She paused with one foot on the step. "What can you tell me about the Finches?"

James didn't meet her eyes. "The Finches are dedicated church members."

Exactly the answer Prentice had expected him to give.

"I'm not trying to alienate you from those who pay your wages. I need information. Three people are dead."

James glanced down at her. His grayish skin crinkled around his dark, beady eyes.

"Not here, of course, but later," she continued. "I can buy you a hot meal."

"You think I'm a renegade?" James's deep voice rumbled.

"No. Renegades don't hang out with doves. You clearly respect Dove Rue."

"Yes, Hawk, I do."

"If you help me, I can resolve this before lies get back to the Order." Prentice got into the carriage. Once she got through the seemingly impenetrable wall of silence in Gould, she could get real answers.

"Destination?" James asked through the carriage's window.

"You choose, since it's about lunch time."

"Yes, Hawk," James replied.

THE OUTER SHELL contained small neighborhoods tucked into various parts of the forested areas of Gould. James took Prentice to once such place with a small restaurant featuring a sloping roof, tight quarters, a roaring hearth, and reeking odor. Vultures flocked to the spot, and carriages, both covered and uncovered, as well as horses tethered along the front crammed the outside lot. Prentice followed James inside, the lunch crowd packing the place to the gills.

James sat in the chair across from Prentice along the windows' edge. She'd managed to find a two-person table that allowed her back to be against the wall while facing the exits in case she need to make a hasty escape. She pulled out her cigarette, lit it, and smoked. That was all she could do to stave off the horrid smell. Carrion. *Blech.*

In a matter of minutes, a man placed a plate of food in front of James. They only had one menu item, and the server didn't bother asking Prentice if she wanted anything. Good thing too, because she didn't eat raw, uncooked things that had been left to decay.

James tore through the carcass with his thick, strong fingers. Blood and flesh squirted beneath his work and oozed out onto the plate. He pushed a gob into his mouth, chewed, and then swallowed. He peered across the metal plate at her.

"The Finches are tenants of the egg, long time."

Prentice smoked and waited.

"We have lived outside the shell for just as long."

She didn't know if "we" meant his family or vultures in general.

"Geraldine Finch had a hardscrabble upbringing that their family's name hid." James ate more of the wretched meat. He moaned softly, caught himself, and cleared his throat.

Prentice closed her eyes and suppressed a shudder. She dug deep to remain patient.

"Illegal work?"

James nodded.

"How come they weren't caught?"

"The shifting sands of business like that benefited the Finches *and* Gould's dark underbelly." James's expression didn't change as he continued. "Plus, Geraldine's a vibrant woman, even now. She runs that household. Few cross her, and those who do, well, they vanish."

"Vanish?"

James nodded. "Rumor is folks end up in the river."

"How has she managed to keep the Order at bay?" Prentice tapped her cigarette on the table's edge. The ashes fell to the floor and joined discarded bones and gristle.

"In her youth, her charm didn't often fall flat. She has a way of homing in on others' weaknesses." James drank his ale.

"Does that include Balthazar?"

James paused. He then lowered his gaze and ate, ripping and tearing the meat with abandon. This continued so long Prentice figured he wouldn't answer.

"She pushed him to the periphery of church affairs but not anymore. Right?" Prentice said.

James continued to ignore her. Clearly, he wouldn't speak ill of his dove, so she switched topics.

"What about Carno Finch?"

James drank a long draft of ale, wiped his mouth with the back of his sleeve, and belched.

"Those are my feelings about him too," Prentice said.

James inclined his head. Vultures had no sense of humor.

"He is the grandchild Geraldine wished Gretchen would have been—obedient. Loyal. Cruel," James said.

"He couldn't inherit the line. He's a male."

"To her that is his only flaw," James said.

"He's the favorite."

Prentice could see it now. Inheritance and power were fed down matriarchal lines. Gretchen, being the first-born daughter of Bella and Oliver would've become the governing head of the Finch household once her grandmother and mother had died. That meant power and wealth as well as reputation.

James chewed, but nodded in affirmation.

Prentice sat back in the wooden chair and smoked. Her mind roiled over the new bits of information. It gave her insights into the Finch family. Balthazar's call-out to her earlier hit home. She *had* been fixated on them and Gretchen. The other two deaths deserved her attention, too, and she'd bet her wings they had connections to what had happened to Gretchen. She just had to figure out *how* they connected.

"There are two more bodies on the green. Did you know that?" Prentice asked James.

In the shadowy corners of this vulture dive, a relaxed and forthcoming James surprised her. He didn't seem to worry about anyone overhearing their conversation. Perhaps their fellow diners had other concerns than about what had happened with their church-loving community members.

"Dove Rue told me yesterday. He said to wait until you said it was okay to remove them."

"Had you seen them before?" Prentice asked. How could the eagles with their sharp eyes and vulture with their affinity for death miss two dead bodies, one burnt to ash and the other a skeleton?

"We routinely clear the grounds of trash and

debris, including the church green. Those bodies didn't appear until Gretchen's body did."

Prentice nodded. Magic. Probably something similar to her *fading* spell. None of the search party spied the bodies until Gretchen's body arrived there. Something broke that spell.

"Once you're done with lunch, I need to go to the eagle's station." Prentice placed a coin on the table that should more than cover lunch and tip for the server.

"Yes, Hawk."

CHAPTER NINE

Eagle Jamison stood on the porch of the security station when Prentice arrived. He was smoking a cigarette. At first, she didn't recognize him, but as she approached, his scent alerted her to his identity.

She stopped at the foot of the stairs. Now that she could see, it surprised her that Jamison had a shaved head and wide-set blue eyes. He had a strong jaw, and his ears were pointed at their ends. The eagles' uniforms were green with yellow stripes along the sides. He had a utility belt around his waist, which included a gun, a knife of some kind, and other items needed to secure and subdue.

"I thought you were coming over this morning," Jamison said by way of greeting.

"I got tied up with other things," Prentice said, still a bit out of sorts by putting Jamison's appearance with the voice and scent she met last night. "The offer's still good, right?"

"Oh yeah. 'Course." He put out his cigarette on the wooden railing and gestured for her to follow him inside.

Inside the station, eagle decor took over. The foundation and walls were built from stone, but the overhead ceiling revealed exposed beams. Wooden floors stretched outward through the structure. Everywhere she looked, she spied eagles working, either hunched over desks writing, some were shelving files and some were talking to citizens. The place had an inviting hum to it. It didn't feel like the eagle stations she'd previously visited. It probably had to do with the fact Gould was such a small egg, and everyone knew everyone else.

"I thought you'd be here earlier, so I had O'Neil set up this little study area for you." He opened the door to a small closet-like room. It had two lanterns lit on a shelf, a metal folding table and matching chair.

"Charming," Prentice said.

"It isn't much, but it's some place quiet where you can sift through reports," Jamison said with a smile. "Look, I'm sorry about last night."

Prentice realized that they stood close together in the doorway's entrance. Jamison was tall, about 6' 2," and had several inches on her. She could feel him breathing. He looked across to her. The look spoke volumes about how he might want to make it up to her.

"Thank you," Prentice said and stepped farther into the room. "Any luck finding Boris or Brian?"

He shook his head. "Alpha unit's out in the outer shell now, knocking on doors and shaking trees."

"You'll let me know when you find them." Prentice made it a statement, not a question.

"Of course. Would you like some tea?" he asked. "It's almost time."

"Sure, and missing persons' reports for the last two weeks."

"Sure thing."

Jamison left, to her relief. Prentice removed the glass containers from her utility belt. She needed to identify them. It looked strange and unnerving to see a person reduced to this—odd bones, teeth, and hair. She couldn't get used to the violence people inflicted upon others.

She slipped them back into their pouch and took out her pad. Over the last three days, she'd taken lots of notes on the case. The eagles' reports arrived on parchment scrolls, tied with leather. The eagle who dropped them off looked like he'd recently been kicked out of the home, barely old enough to work.

"Here you go, Hawk Tasifa," he said with a strong blush and a wobbly cadence.

"You are...?" Prentice took the scrolls.

"Eagle Smith."

"It's nice to meet you. Will you shut the door as you leave?"

"Yes, Hawk." He bowed and bolted through the door.

Prentice didn't think she looked *that* intimidating. She chuckled and got settled at the desk. It held deep scars from writing instruments and what looked like frequent re-locations. The tiny space had a window right above the desk, and she could look out on the pathway that ran in front of the station.

Four scrolls. Four missing persons in Gould in the last couple of weeks. That couldn't be right. Could it? She took the first scroll, loosened its tie, and unrolled it. The report date was Robin 23rd, two weeks before Prentice arrived in Gould. She'd arrived the early evening of Canari 1st.

According to the report, a rooster named Alicia Redfern had gone missing. Last seen on the 22nd. Her mother, a Mary Ann Redfern, had filed the report. Prentice had picked up a bit about Gould neighborhoods. Alicia's address was in the outer shell in Coopertino. Where she worked snared Prentice's attention. *Dale's Coop*.

She made a note in her pad. She wanted to go back to Dale's and ask around. She didn't want to disturb Alicia's mom without having anything to give her in return. If she had to guess, the skeleton on the green was Alicia. The illustration of her depicted a pretty woman, blond hair with only a few scars along her cheek and forehead. She had one beneath her eye, which she had turned into a flower, complete with pink petals. The only other facial scar was along the corner of her lip, where a nail must've hooked her mouth. Alicia had tattooed stars from the injury up to her cheek in a starburst.

Prentice scribbled her notes and then went to the next scroll. There she found another missing woman, Tammy Jo Greer. She didn't work at Dale's. Nothing had been written in the employer spot. One thing caught Prentice's attention. Tammy Jo also lived in Coopertino. The illustration depicted a heavy-set woman with a round face, thick with scars along the left side of that face. She wore her hair in chunky braids with bright red tips. Silver piercings decorated her scars.

Prentice found her pretty. Her wife reported her missing. She also had three chicks. A mom, a wife, and a missing person. Prentice wrote down the information to ask Dale and Darlene about later, before visiting Tammy Jo's wife. She didn't want to upset the families.

Her disappearance happened earlier than Alicia's, which meant Prentice had to revise her timeline. She crossed out information and updated her notes. She rolled the report up and secured it. She did the same for Alicia's report. Two more reports remained. One had to be Gretchen's. She had a strange feeling in her feathers. None of these women knew how close they came to danger until it was too late.

Thumping hard against the door, Jamison made his way in. His arms held a teapot, a teacup, sugar, and milk, all on a tray. He offered a crooked smile. "Tea!"

Prentice glanced up from her notes. "Great."

He looked at her desk, and then the tray. "I'll put this over here." He set the tray down on the floor beside the desk.

"Thank you."

"You have any questions?" Jamison leaned against the wall, blocking the door.

"Tell me about the Coopertino neighborhood." Prentice shifted in the seat to look at him.

He shrugged thick shoulders. "It's in the outer shell. Mostly residential area occupied by roosters, though there are a few crows who live there too. Outside of the pecking order fights and general domestic situations, it's not a bad area. We don't get many calls to go out there. They tend to take care of things themselves."

"Two of the four reports for missing persons are from Coopertino." Prentice pointed to the two scrolls.

Jamison shrugged again. "We figured they were runaways."

"Tammy Jo has a wife and children. She's not some rebellious teen. People don't often walk away from that without divorce. Parents want to be near their children."

"Tammy Jo had a difficult marriage. We got calls to come out there and settle their domestics a few times. We figured she ran off and she didn't want to be found. Maybe she left to cool off and think. You know? We thought she'd be back." Jamison stared down at the floor.

"She's been missing since Robin 18th." Prentice shook her head.

"I did assign an eagle to investigate and follow up. I can check with her," he said. "She may have an update."

"You do that." Prentice turned back to the desk and selected the next scroll. She heard the door close behind her.

The next scroll was indeed Gretchen's. Prentice didn't glean any additional information than she had from the family and Balthazar. The dates aligned to what she'd been told and what she had read in the request Balthazar sent the Order. She quickly rolled it back up and placed it on the pile with the others.

Three.

The final scroll held two names: Boris and Brian Greer. Cousins to Tammy Jo. They worked at the local timber company as loggers. Both men were last seen on Robin 30th, the day after Gretchen went missing and a day before her body was found. Their parents reported them missing. They also lived in

Coopertino. That's four people who had gone missing in the last two weeks.

It wasn't a coincidence.

It was a pattern.

Prentice wrote down the information in her pad. She stood up and stretched. Outside, the daylight faded. She groaned, stretching her wings in the tight space. She'd been reviewing and working for well over an hour and a half.

She opened the door and stepped out into the hallway. The busy station had calmed. Those who'd come in during lunch had left. She found Jamison at the front desk, talking to a man seated there. She recognized him as Eagle Smith, and she waved as she approached.

"Hello," Prentice said.

Jamison turned around and so did Eagle Smith, who shot out of his chair.

"Are you finished already?" Jamison asked.

"I'm done with the reports. Thank you for letting me review them. Can I speak to you, in private, Eagle Jamison?"

"Of course."

He followed her back down to the closet-sized room. She shut the door behind them.

"Four people missing from Coopertino. All roosters. That's a pattern and a problem, Eagle Jamison. All within two weeks. You should have daily patrols down there." Prentice fought to keep her voice level.

Jamison rounded on her, his face a mask of anger. "You aren't going to come here and tell me how to patrol my egg!"

"I wouldn't have to if you didn't have four people missing and one confirmed dead girl!"

Jamison hissed. "I told you. We're investigating it."

Prentice said, "And while you drag your feathers, people will continue to die."

With that she collected her items. She thought about telling Jamison about the two bodies on the green, but she didn't want to tip her hand yet. Not until she had full confirmation about the victims' identities. She couldn't trust him or the rest of the eagles to be smart about identification.

Jamison collected the reports. He left without a word. She heard him farther down the hall demand Smith to come collect the tea tray. She left without another word to either of them. As she walked out of the station, she found James seated on the stairs. He had a glass of water in his fist, and his usual expressionless face pointed toward the horizon.

"Ready, Hawk Tasifa?" he asked, getting to his feet.

"Call me Prentice."

"Yes, Hawk Tasifa."

She got into the carriage and pondered what she'd learned.

"Destination?"

"Carlita Starbucks."

"Yes, Hawk Tasifa."

Prentice laughed. "James!"

The carriage door locked, and it rocked gently as James climbed into the driver's seat. The reins snapped and the horse pulled forward, carrying them out onto the path and along their way. As they pulled away, she spied Eagle Jamison come out onto the porch and watch them.

She could see his cigarette smoke drifting into the air.

CHAPTER TEN

About thirty minutes later, Prentice knocked rapidly on Carlita's door. The doorknob jiggled from the opposite side, but it didn't open.

"It's me. Open up, Carlita."

The door opened, and Carlita hugged themselves. Dressed in a long black dress with short sleeves and a high collar with boots, they appeared to be grieving. Their long dark hair had been pulled into a high ponytail, held by a silver and diamond clasp. Chunky silver bangles adorned their wrists.

"What do you want?" They didn't meet Prentice's eyes, but tears stained their cheeks.

"I needed some fresh air, and I'm here about Alicia Redfern."

Carlita frowned. "The waitress at Dale's Coop?"

"Yes."

"Has something happened?" Carlita fell back

enough to allow Prentice to enter their home. The treehouse had been tidied since Prentice's last visit. The leather loveseat now faced the leather chair adjacent to the stone fireplace. Lanterns sat in equal measure on the mantle. Shiny and colorful vases gleamed beside the glowing lanterns.

"She's dead," Prentice said as she closed the door behind her.

Carlita gasped. They walked into the living room, picked up their throw pillow, and collapsed into the chair. They gestured for Prentice to sit across from them. A thick tree stump made a makeshift table. A bone-white teacup sat with steaming liquid inside. A saucer contained a partially eaten sandwich.

"She was so ordinary," Carlita said, drawing Prentice's attention back to them.

"What does that mean?" Prentice asked as she came over and took a proffered seat across from them.

"She was like everyone else. Hustling hard. Trying to enjoy her life."

"Did you see a lot of her at the Coop?" Prentice asked, leaning forward, resting her elbows on her knees.

"We didn't go to Dale's all the time, so not really." Carlita picked up the teacup with one hand and held the throw pillow tight in the other.

"You ever see Carno at the Coop?" Prentice asked.

"Gretchen's brother?"

Prentice nodded.

"Only twice, maybe. One time he came down there angry at Gretchen. They argued something furious."

"About?"

Carlita shrugged. "Dunno. There was loud music, shouting, and whatnot."

Having been to Dale's, Prentice understood. "Go on."

"After a period of sulking and being surly, he tried flirting with one of the hens there. He ended up manhandling her until they went outside."

"What happened to the woman?" Prentice asked, having a good idea of where this was heading. It didn't surprise her Carno had tried to force his way. He had weak character. The goddess wouldn't approve.

Carlita hugged the pillow close. "Hens can be mean. Which is why you shouldn't mess with them. When Carno came back inside, he had scratches all over his face and neck, if we remember correctly."

"What did he do then?" Prentice wrote notes down in her pad.

Carlita fingered the pillow's tassels. "Dunno. He stormed off to the restroom or something. Gretchen used to say Carno got volatile when he didn't get his way, so he got mouthy with the hen again and Dale tossed him out."

Carlita unknowingly had witnessed Carno attacking a woman.

"Was the woman Alicia?" Prentice asked.

Carlita cast their eyes on the fire. "No. I think this was a few days before Alicia left."

Alicia left. Prentice didn't show it on her face, but she found it strange. Carlita had alluded to Alicia leaving as if on a trip or vacation. Prentice wondered who had spun that narrative. She'd have to go down to Dale's and follow up. They could shed more light on who might have hurt Gretchen and the others.

"Can you tell me how Gretchen reacted that night?"

Carlita chuckled. "She blew it off. She was with Boris. Oblivious."

Prentice thought about how a young woman in her first real relationship would be happy to be rid of her overbearing brother. So, she decided to switch gears.

"How did Gretchen feel about her family?"

"She was irritated with them, and she loved them." Carlita sipped her tea.

"But…"

"But, Carno scared her. He was a dark person. You understand? You could sense he was capable of hurt." Carlita shuddered. "There never seemed to be a real person in there. But I've only met him two or three times."

Did something darker lurk beneath Carno's

attractive façade? Prentice had seen the mask slip and the real monster peek out when she reviewed their limited interactions. His arguments with his grandmother had seemed over the top.

"Why didn't you tell me this before?" Prentice asked, shaking her head.

"You dunno how powerful the Finch family is in Gould. Plus, our best friend had been killed. We were numb, shocked, and we didn't know if we were next. We still don't know." Carlita wiped their eyes. "Our stomach bubbled, and we were shaking and sweaty…"

"I'm sorry. You're right to be cautious. I'm sorry for your loss."

Carlita sobbed. "She wanted someone to fill the void inside her. She was so lonely. That's all."

In a home filled with family, Gretchen shouldn't have been lonely.

"Thank you for your time. I will be in touch." Prentice stood.

Carlita had curled up into the chair, and sipped their tea, lost in the dancing flames.

JAMES HAD FED the horse while Prentice interviewed Carlita. His expression didn't change when she emerged. He only nodded in greeting. She got the carriage steps down herself and climbed in without waiting for James. Her conversation with Carlita had left her much to ponder. The sun hugged the horizon, and her stomach grumbled for food. She closed her eyes.

"Would you like to return to the church now, Hawk Tasifa?" James's deep rumble asked.

"Yes, please. I'm sure the dove wants you back. I've taken you from your chores most of the day."

"My brother is there today," James replied.

"No wonder he was so adamant I take the carriage. He must've wanted me out of his hair." Prentice laughed.

James grunted.

"You don't have to agree with him."

Soon the carriage started on its way. She'd gotten used to the swaying and bumpy ride through Gould's streets and pathways. James had lowered the windows, so the forest's sweet smell wafted in. Beneath those odors came the river's earthiness and the flush of floral aromas.

She awoke to James unlocking the carriage door. Darkness had descended, and her muscles felt stiff from the awkward angle she'd slept in. Rubbing her neck, she stepped out of the carriage.

To her surprise, Balthazar didn't come out to greet her. As she looked around, carriages filled the lot, all arranged in neat rows. Music and voices drifted from the church's sanctuary.

"It's Wednesday evening services." James

answered her unspoken question. "Good night, Hawk Tasifa."

She'd lost track of the days.

"Good evening, James."

Prentice headed through the courtyard and into the side hallway that led to the dove's office and the spiral staircase up to the living quarters. She went into the guest room and found the fire lit and fresh fruit placed on the table beside her bed. It confirmed what she suspected. James maintained contact with the dove.

She'd debrief the dove in the morning. Right now, she was starving. She picked up an apple and bit into it. A folded piece of parchment sealed with the dove's symbol rested on her bed. Prentice opened it to find a message from Balthazar.

Prentice—

I also asked Dr. Little to come up and examine those remains as you requested. She arrived just after you left. I believe she spent the greater part of the afternoon back there on the green. She said she'd have findings for you soon. The remains have been removed.

"Thank you!" Prentice said to the letter.

While she ate, she took out her notes and re-read them. It bothered her that so many people had disappeared and the eagles didn't find it necessary to investigate. Sure, roosters didn't line the church's pocket with birdsong, but they deserved basic empathy.

Moving on, she took out the glass container of bones and teeth and the second glass container with the hair. She sat on the floor and removed parchment from one of her pouches, unfolding it and securing it on the floor with heavier objects at the corners, her notepad, one of her boots at the other end. Next, she drew a circle on the page and divided it into four quadrants. She wrote the names of each of the missing people, one in each area.

Then she removed her dowsing pendulum. It featured a hawk that rested at the end of a silver chain. Prentice removed her pen dagger from its sheath on her utility belt. It bit into her index finger and she wiped the blood across the casting stone's talons.

She whispered, "*Determiner.*"

She opened the glass jar and held the stone above the bones and teeth. Once she had counted until ten, she moved the pendulum above the names on the parchment. She continued to chant the word. The room bled away, leaving only herself and the parchment. The pendulum swung around the names and, as it slowed, it settled on the name Prentice had believed the burnt ashes to belong to all along.

Alicia Redfern. Her spiritual essence rose from the parchment with a moan. She drifted into the ceiling and vanished.

To confirm the skeletal remains' identity, Prentice removed the jar and opened it.

"Determiner."

Just as it did with Alicia's remains, the pendulum swung toward Tammy Jo's name etched on the parchment.

Exhausted, Prentice croaked, "*Fin.*"

She closed her eyes, and when she opened them again, she'd returned to the guest room. From the clock, only fifteen minutes had passed. Prentice cleaned the pendulum and her pen dagger in the bathroom sink. She placed her things away and hung up her utility belt.

Prentice made herself a drink of warm tea, crafted from Lanham leaves, water from the bathroom's tap, and her own conjured flame. She held it close, allowing its warmth to seep into her body, chasing away the cold indifference she found in death. She sipped and pulled the blankets over her legs.

Prentice could feel the case drawing close, and as the pieces came together, she knew the next few steps would be the most difficult. She stretched her wings and wrapped them around herself.

Tomorrow would come soon enough.

Prentice drifted off to sleep.

CHAPTER ELEVEN

The clear morning sky held the night's chill as the sun crested the horizon. Birds chirped and roused Prentice from her sleep. She stared at the ceiling beams. They stretched the length of the room and cradled shadows cast by the low fire's flames. She pushed herself to a sitting position. An empty glass, an extinguished candle, and her notepad littered the tiny table beside the bed. Groaning, she got out of bed. She went to her utility belt and removed her cigarettes. Only two remained. With another groan, she stuck one of the remaining two into her mouth and held it in her teeth.

As she lit the tip, someone knocked on her door. She inhaled. *Who the heck is awake this early?* The clock gave the time as 6:12.

"It's me. Balthazar. May I enter?"

Prentice grabbed her cloak and wrapped it around her nudity. "Come."

Balthazar came in dressed in a long black cloak embroidered with the goddess's sigil in golden threads. Long sleeves peeked out from beneath the cloak and he lowered the hood. In one hand, he held a steaming bowl and in the other a glass of what appeared to be sweet milk.

"How did you know I was up?" she asked, holding her cloak closed and smoking. Not for the first time did she suspect the dove spied on her.

"I didn't, but I hoped you remembered we're releasing Gretchen to the sky today." He placed the bowl and the milk on the fireplace mantel. The ceremony is at eight."

"No one mentioned it to me."

Balthazar frowned. "If you want to attend, we'll be on the church green where her nest is already being set up. Eight o'clock. Molly has already placed a clean towel and soap in the bathroom for you."

"It sounds like I don't have a choice."

"It would be best for you to attend, as a representative of the Order."

Prentice blew out a stream of frustration with her smoke. She didn't like morning, but she did want to do right by Gretchen, the strong-willed daughter who didn't feel a need to conform. She rebelled against the confines of the small egg and indulged her wild heart, only to be killed for it. All her plans came to abrupt and violent end.

"Thank you for breakfast," Prentice said. "I'll be down."

Relief made Balthazar's face handsome again. "Thank you. I have to go prepare. See you then."

He left, shutting the door quietly behind him. She locked it. She took the sweet milk and the bowl of oats to her bed and sat down cross-legged, allowing her cloak to fan out around her. Rolled oats had been a childhood treat. She would add honey and nuts to sweeten and give it crunch. But here, she had none of those, so she poured some of her sweet milk into the bowl, stirred with the spoon, and ate the first bite.

"Oh, this is good." She shuddered in pleasure.

Realization that she hadn't had a good, solid meal the day before hit her like a stone. Within minutes she'd devoured the breakfast and had started on one of the apples from the bowl of fruit provided last night. She drained the last of the sweet milk. Next, she crafted a cup of Lanham tea. One check of her tea and tobacco supplies reinforced that she needed to slow down their consumption. She didn't know how long she'd be in Gould.

Full, Prentice added two more logs to the fire, fanned the flames a bit, and removed her cloak. She wanted the room warm when she returned from the bath. She started the water with relief, thankful the guest room had an adjoining bath with running water. Sure enough, Molly had placed fresh towels and soap in the room, probably yesterday. It was as neat as a pin.

Prentice had been too tired to pay much attention. In the wee hours of the morning, she had used the toilet, washed her hands, and sleepily returned to bed.

Now awake, she saw the detail Molly had gone through to decorate and make the guest room inviting and comfortable. Rather than view it as an invasion of privacy, Prentice saw the attempt to make her feel welcome. Fresh, fragrant flowers sprouted from colored vases that adorned the shelves above the sink. The claw-foot tub had a spout where water poured into it. Above the tub, a round window complete with a wooden cross in its center allowed in sunlight. A plush fur rug, probably from a fox, lay in front of the tub. The floor's wood warmed in the early morning rays.

While the tub filled, Prentice looked through her satchel for something suitable to wear to a funeral. Somber events, funerals held at court were also opportunities for everyone to wear their best clothes. She doubted it would be any different here. She removed her more decorative head-wrap. This one was ebony and gold, like Balthazar's cloak. She would wear this one today, along with her black pants and dark green shirt. Her cloak, with its scarlet red, would stand out in the crowd, but that couldn't be helped. Hawks were meant to be seen, the color a warning of their presence.

Prentice stopped the water and got in the tub. She lowered herself down into the warm waters and sighed in sweet relief. At court, showers ruled. No one had time for luxury baths, except for the cardinals and falcons. They resided in the upper floors of the birdhouse. The rest, like Prentice—condors and hawks, rooks and the rest—resided in various apartments throughout Lanham Egg.

She closed her eyes and used her feathers to push the water around her body. In a few minutes, she'd use the soap and water to bathe in earnest, but now, she wanted to simply enjoy this moment of quiet bliss.

She thought back to her apartment in Lanham. It didn't contain much more than this guest room. Not that she enjoyed a minimalist life, but she did journey to other nests on assignment. Her residence looked more like a storage unit than an actual home. Despite that, it did contain her favorite things and it was *hers.* She'd been able to place wards about her home and when there, she felt completely safe.

Here, in Gould, she didn't feel safe. An ever-creeping dread stained the sun-drenched days and cool nights. Something bad had happened here. It was *still* happening here. She shook her feathers, and the water sprayed across the walls, the floor, and the window.

Prentice laughed. "Whoops!"

She took the cloth and the soap from the sink and dunked them in the water. She began to lather and then applied the soapy cloth to her skin, cleaning her arms first. As she did so, she hummed another Tisonian song her mother had taught her.

THE IRONY of Gretchen's funeral being conducted on the very grounds where they discovered her body wasn't lost on Prentice. She arrived as what appeared to be the whole of Gould turned out to send Gretchen to the sky.

Rows of folding wooden chairs had been placed farther down the green. In the center, a large circular nest had been constructed from wooden sticks and logs. It had been covered with a black, sheer veil, and from this distance, Prentice made out a body inside the nest. When women go into labor, they were placed inside a nest, filled with feathers and blankets. As people were born into the world, so shall they return to the goddess. Today, Gretchen would get to soar.

Vultures dressed in long black robes acted as the funeral attendants. This practice didn't differ from the other nests Prentice had visited. She watched them escort people to seats. Two attendants stood alert at the front of the burial nest. Beside them torches burned. A total of five torches had been lit. Balthazar came to stand between the two vultures at the entrance to the nest.

Prentice found a seat at the back. She wanted to be able to slip out if necessary as well as watch everyone else.

The Finch family arrived to a rustling of murmurs and cries. A gaunt Bella carried herself with a quiet determination that proclaimed to all they wouldn't see her fall apart. She wore a dark veil, an elaborate hat, and a flowing pantsuit cinched at the waist with a floral scarf and black boots.

Her husband, Oliver, was another story. The mild-mannered man buckled under the weight of his grief. He collapsed to the ground when the two vulture attendants removed the veil over the nest. He looked broken. His daughters helped him to the seats at the front.

The three girls wore similar pants ensembles to their mother's, but instead of a veil, they wore dark, wide-brimmed hats decorated with flowers. Carno brought up the rear. He wore dark glasses, but Prentice knew his demons lay just beneath the surface. His performances about Gretchen felt false and forced. His demeanor was off. His angst had come out of left field on both occasions. She didn't buy his act. Why was he trying so hard to get her to think he hated his sister?

One of the funeral attendants reached out to help Geraldine to her seat.

"Get off! Don't touch me!" She reeled away from the attendant's outstretched hand.

He fell back and waited for her and Robert to view their granddaughter and then shuffle on to their seats. There were no words exchanged between Geraldine and her daughter. There were tensions beneath the surface. The period of blind faith Bella had in her mother might have come to an end. Bella's sister, Skylar, her husband, and toddlers completed the family's arrival and they all consumed the front row before the nest.

"Everyone, please, take your seats, quickly and quietly," Balthazar said from the front. When he spoke, a calm descended over the crowd. People who had gone up to view Gretchen, some openly weeping, returned to their seats.

Prentice spied Carlita sitting toward the back, farther down the row from her. She scanned the crowd, but she didn't see any roosters. Surely Boris and Brian wouldn't miss the funeral. That puzzled her. Boris should've been there. Unless he couldn't face what he'd done to her.

"Let us pray." Balthazar launched into the goddess's prayer of wings.

All bowed their heads, but Prentice scanned the

group. Bella and Oliver were devoted to each other. They indulged their children's every whim. Even now, Prentice could tell in the way both parents touched their daughters and held them, spoke to them in soft, gentle tones. There was love there. She felt heartsick for Bella.

"Hoot," Balthazar said, looking up from his prayer.

"Hoot," the crowd echoed.

"Sometimes, goodbye is a second chance. An opportunity to reflect on the joys and happy memories and on our own flight path," Balthazar said, holding his hands pressed together. He hooked his thumbs and spread out his palms in the goddess wings. "Today, we are here to launch Gretchen to her eternal home in the sky, so her beautiful soul can soar once more."

Oliver's shallow breathing turned into hiccups. He trembled with sorrow and cried a flood beside his wife. The girls wept too, and Prentice spied Rachel hugging her older sister close, their heads together. Carno remained stoic. Geraldine and Robert could've been statues— blank faces, no tears, no emotion, nothing. Bella's cheek looked wet from tears. From Prentice's position, she couldn't be sure.

A storm of emotions permeated the atmosphere. It all exploded when Balthazar ended his prayer and gestured for Bella to come up. Once she reached him, he passed one of the torches to her, and she walked up to the nest where her eldest daughter lay. She whispered something, wiped her cheek, and set her torch to the nest's wood. It ignited the paper kindling stuffed throughout the nest.

Bella returned to her seat, back straight, head held high. Oliver passed her on the way to the nest, and his hand visibly trembled as a vulture handed him a torch. He collapsed to his knees, away from the flames. His sobs superseded the flames' crackling, but he slowly put his torch into the nest's wood.

Smoke billowed into the crisp blue sky. One of the attendants had to help Oliver back to his seat. Next, Carno strolled to the nest, snatched one of the torches from the attendant, and threw it in without a second thought. Cries of shock broke through the tense quiet, and he sniggered as he returned to the first row. He must've been the siblings' representative, because the next people to get up where Geraldine and Robert. They shuffled to the now burning nest, accepting their torch from Balthazar without comment. They stood quietly a short distance back from the nest before throwing the torch into the flames. Skylar and her husband received the fifth and final torch, and they threw it into the already roaring flames.

Balthazar raised his arms and gestured for everyone to stand.

"Gretchen Finch, we send you to the sky, to soar for all eternity. Let us begin."

He launched into *Wings of Sorrow, Soaring High*, and the crowd joined him. They watched the nest burn, its flames eagerly licking the air, greedily consuming the nest.

It burned hot and fast.

Just like Gretchen.

CHAPTER TWELVE

Later that day, Prentice entered Dale's Coop at lunch time. It drew a sizable crowd. Scattered feed on the floor crunched beneath Prentice's boots. It smelled like roasted corn, whiskey, and cigarette smoke. As soon as Dale spied her walking in, he shouted to Darlene with a toss of his colorful mane.

"Aye, Darlene!" Once he got her attention, he went back to serving drinks at the bar.

Darlene looked to the entrance and waved at Prentice. Most of the folks stuffed into the coop didn't pay much attention to her and she found that relaxing. It meant she didn't have to conjure any magic to move about the place. As she made her way to the area where Darlene was serving patrons, Prentice noticed the diverse lunch crowd. She spied some crows, a few ravens, and what appeared to be a swan seated in the back. His long neck and flowing white-gold hair glowed against the shadows.

The feed must be really good here, Prentice thought.

People could visit and be themselves here. Privacy and service were hard to find in many parts of the kingdom.

"Hiya!" Darlene greeted Prentice once in earshot.

"When do you go on break? I need to talk to you." Prentice kept her voice low.

Darlene stuck her serving tray underneath her arm. Her facial scars bore bright green curlicues and hearts. She wore a matching green tank-top and short brown shorts that showed off her long, muscular legs. She had thick thighs that tested the shorts' fabric strength.

"I don't know nothing else to tell you."

"It's about Alicia and Tammy Jo," Prentice said, dropping her voice even lower. It forced Darlene to lean in to hear her.

As she pulled back, Darlene's face had paled. She nodded numbly and mumbled, "Go on to the kitchen. I'll be right there."

Prentice headed to the kitchen. She heard Darlene shout to Dale that she needed ten minutes. Despite being packed and busy, other servers floated among the crowd. Maybe one of them could cover for Darlene. One thing Prentice knew for sure: Darlene ran Dale's Coop.

"Aye, no patrons!" shouted a red-faced rooster. He wore a green apron over his tee-shirt and pants. He also had a mask, a hairnet, and a towel tossed over his shoulder. "You deaf?"

The feed browned in the skillet. Bowls filled with various food awaited delivery. A server rushed by Prentice with a fast "coming through," scooped up several of the bowls in a feat that amazed her, and zipped right back out.

"Darlene told me to come back here," Prentice said.

"Go on back to the office, then. Make a right. Yeah. That way. All the way down to the end of the hall."

She couldn't tell from the front of the building the coop had so much additional space. Prentice followed the cook's directions and ended up outside a tiny, cramped office. She didn't go in, but rather hung around the door, waiting. Besides, the space only had room enough for one body to sit down. A heavy ledger lay open, and it filled much of the desk's surface. On the floor, a basket stuffed with rolled scrolls spilled over.

"Sorry about that," Darlene said as she walked down the narrow hallway to the office. She went in and sat down at the desk. No one else could enter the space with the ledger, boxes, and files. She hunched against the desk and took out a cigarette. "You mind?"

"No." Prentice shook her head.

"Cloves."

Soon the sweetened aroma meshed with the kitchen's greasy odor.

"So, what about Alicia and Tammy Jo?" Darlene asked.

"They're dead."

"What?"

"Dead. I can't tell you more details because it's an active investigation, but both women are dead. I need you to tell me about the last time you saw each of them with Carno Finch." Prentice took out her pencil and pad.

Darlene smoked. She shuddered as she spoke. "Carno Finch."

"Yeah."

She rolled her eyes and shook her head. "He'd come down here some nights lookin' for his sister. We don't get a lot of the g-crowd around here."

"The g-crowd?"

"Goddess crowd."

Prentice smirked.

"That's why I remember," Darlene said. "He raised all kinds of ruckus. But then he saw Alicia workin'. I guess he took a likin' to her. She didn't return it. You know how it is."

Prentice nodded. "I'm assuming he didn't take her rejection well."

Darlene shook her head. "Strange that. You

know? When she brushed him off, the devil shone in his eyes. He threatened to sow our fields with salt."

Prentice winced. Everyone depended on their vegetable crops. Threatening to sabotage one's fields couldn't be discounted or overlooked as jest.

"What happened next?"

"Alicia said he had a pleasant lookin' face, but behind the mask, he was just weird. She told me she let 'im down gently, you know, and he wandered off. That's the last we saw of 'im around here. We got busy that night."

"Did you see Alicia afterward?"

Tears leaked out and Darlene sobbed. "No. Dale said she probably ran off with Brian. People come and go all the time 'round here."

"No one has seen Boris, either," Prentice said.

"No. What's happening to us?" Darlene broke down completely.

"I'm going to find out, Darlene. I'm going to put this right."

Darlene looked at her. "Thank you."

"Thank you for being frank and honest with me. Now, can you tell me about Tammy Jo and the time Carno got tossed out?"

Darlene recounted the events much the same as Carlita, with one new tidbit. When Tammy Jo came back inside from her scuffle with Carno, she looked dazed and she had dirt or earth along her face. Darlene helped her wash off the stinging substance.

Earth magic, if Darlene had to guess.

She thanked Darlene again. "You have my caller?"

"Yes."

"Contact me any time."

Darlene nodded and wiped her eyes with the palms of her hands. She continued smoking.

"Can you find your way out? I'm gonna be a moment."

"Yes, I can." Prentice patted Darlene's shoulder and left.

She joined James outside on the stoop. "Did you get anything to eat?"

James shook his head. "Not my kind of place."

"Right. I remember. If you can drop me off at the Finches', you can go grab lunch," Prentice said. She paused. "There are places in the egg to get carrion. Right?"

James nodded. "Yes, Hawk Tasifa."

They left the coop. The brutality of what had happened to these women churned her stomach. Carno liked being in control and getting what he wanted, and he had wanted Alicia. So, he stole her.

Prentice could feel in her feathers that she was right. Carno hadn't committed one heinous act but three. All the people in Gould were in grave danger, both in the egg and in the outer shell.

Nearly an hour later, Rachel met Prentice at the gate. "Hawk Tasifa!"

"Greetings, Rachel." Prentice waved. "Are your parents in?"

"Yes, they're expecting you. Dove Rue called earlier this morning to let them know you wanted a meeting."

She'd left a note for Balthazar asking him to set up an early afternoon meeting with Bella and Oliver only. Prentice needed to talk to Gretchen's parents. She'd thought of having them come down to the church and conducting the interview in Balthazar's study, but that would draw more attention than Prentice wanted. She also wanted the Finches to be relaxed. If she came to them, that would make them less tense and nervous especially after the funeral.

"Is your grandmother home?" Prentice asked as she walked through the open gate.

Rachel busily re-chained and closed the lock. She deposited the key in her dress pocket. "No, she and Carno went out shopping, down to the Apothecary."

She took Muffin by the reins, and they walked beside Prentice toward the Finch home.

"How are things?" Prentice asked.

"Strange," Rachel said, and then caught herself. "I mean, they're fine."

"I see."

Rachel nodded and they walked the half-mile up to the house in silence.

Once they reached the house, just as before, the butler met Prentice and took her inside. Rachel disappeared around back to return Muffin to the horse barn.

Without the pain and over extension of her hawk abilities, Prentice could make out the normal view of the Finches' home. They didn't go straight into the grand room that overlooked the river but made a left down a shorter corridor. This one was lined with a rug that ran the length of the hall. Oil paintings of the river and various stages of the Finch home decorated the walls on both sides. Only one door on the left, and it stood ajar.

The butler gestured Prentice to enter. "You will find Madam Finch and her husband in the library."

Prentice entered the room, and the door clicked shut behind her.

Library was the perfect word for this room. It took up two floors, with a large, boxy stone fireplace at the opposite end of the room from the door. Here too were warm, ornate rugs, sweeping candelabras made of gold and brass, and lanterns crafted to match the décor.

Shelves covered every available wall space on both floors. On each side of the room, spiral staircases led up to the second floor of the library where even more shelves crammed with books awaited eager, ravenous readers. Statues of the goddess—her wings extended in flight, her perched on a live branch, and other depictions—stood in near life-sized beauty in the corners. It smelled of dust, old magic, and burnt wood.

"Wow," Prentice said.

"That's why this is our favorite room," Bella Finch said, coming toward Prentice from the space closest to the fire. "My family has been collecting rare books—and some illegal—for centuries."

Prentice nodded, too stunned at the expanse and beauty of the library to say more. She moved to meet Bella halfway, and the two came together at the library's center. Bella shook her hand.

"It's good to see you again. When you left last time, we were concerned about your well-being."

"Thank you. I'm fine."

Prentice followed Bella back to where Oliver waited, standing beside a settee positioned in from of the fire. Once she reached him, Prentice greeted him as well.

"Please sit, Hawk Tasifa, and tell us what this is about," Bella said, sitting down. Oliver sat beside her and, as instructed, Prentice sat in the armchair across from them.

"I appreciate you seeing me. I have a few more questions, and I wanted to get answers to them from you without distractions," Prentice explained. She removed her pad and pencil and scooted to the chair's edge.

"Okay." Bella bit her lower lip, a habit Prentice had seen in young Rachel.

"Is there new information you can tell us?" Oliver asked.

"Not at this time, but I can tell you I am close to identifying who killed your daughter." Prentice looked them in the eyes.

Oliver gasped. "So quickly? Wow."

Bella narrowed her eyes at Prentice. "She said she was close, Ollie."

"Right. That's where you come in." Prentice offered a soft smile meant to put them at ease.

"Go ahead. Ask your questions." Bella sat back on the settee.

"Tell me about your reaction to learning Gretchen was dating a rooster." Prentice had to start with the hardest question. She didn't know if they knew, but she assumed they did. Carno knew and he wouldn't have kept it secret.

Bella let out a long sigh. "We didn't overreact, but we were admittedly concerned."

"About the relationship?"

Bella whispered, "Yes."

"So, you both knew she was courting Boris?"

Oliver said, "Yes. We didn't agree. She knew that, but she was smitten. We believed she'd get tired of it soon and end it."

"Did everyone feel that way about it? That it was

just a phase?" Prentice knew the answer, but she had to ask to get confirmation.

"The girls didn't seem to mind. I mean, we tried to focus so much of our energy on the positive," Bella said.

"As the goddess teaches," Oliver interjected.

"Hoot," Prentice said.

"Hoot," the Finches echoed.

Oliver burst into tears.

A few quiet moments passed. He removed a handkerchief.

"And Carno?" Prentice asked.

"Carno's so meticulous. He's the opposite of Gretchen, who liked things messy and spontaneous," Bella confessed with a chuckle. "They were polar opposites."

"Was it Carno who told you about Gretchen's relationship with Boris?"

"Yes. I was frantic. He had gone out to find her one evening when she missed her curfew. The next morning, he came down to breakfast. He had several scratches, a bite mark, I think, and other injuries. He said he fell grooming the horses, but then he told us about Boris." Bella swallowed what sounded like tears.

"And you believed him?"

Bella put her head in her hands. "Yes, of course. We asked Gretchen, and she bristled underneath his strict expectations of her. As the oldest daughter, she was next in line to govern the Finch clan."

"That was the night before Gretchen went missing."

Bella nodded.

"I suspect the gulf between Gretchen and Carno came to a head and he killed her," Prentice said.

Bella's head snapped up. "No!"

"I know it's difficult to hear," Prentice started.

"Over the last few months, Carno's been descending into something else," Oliver said, pulling his wife into his embrace. "By the goddess, he came home like nothing had happened."

"I believed him completely, but I—I had a bad feeling in my stomach," Bella said.

Oliver hugged her tight. "Perhaps you should go, Hawk."

"Thank you for your time." Prentice stood, putting away her pad and pencil as she did so.

Oliver stood too. Like a cloud, he followed her to the library door. Seconds before he closed it after her, Bella released a horrible scream. It carried so much anguish and grief that Prentice readily fled.

It would haunt her for years to come.

CHAPTER THIRTEEN

Prentice made her way back down the hallway. She made the right, into the corridor that led to the front door. Her feathers rustled in warning. Before she could turn around—a flash of pain struck her—her knees buckled. Her feet gave way. She looked up from the floor to see Carno hovering over her, gloating.

"Can't see everything, can you?" He laughed.

He couldn't help himself. His true nature showed. The pain flared at the base of her neck. She reached up to the spot, feeling a sizable knot. Her fingers touched something wet.

Great. Blood.

"*Immobile*," Carno said and sprinkled dirt across her body. The word flew out fast and furious.

She tried to reach for her talons but found herself

unable to move her arms or legs. All the air had been sucked from her lungs.

"Don't just stand there grinning like a hyena. We have to move her."

Prentice laughed at her own naivete.

Carno killed Gretchen. That angle that didn't seem plausible without help.

He started moving, putting a blindfold over Prentice's eyes, securing her hands and feet. A lump formed in her throat. Her mouth dried like she'd chewed cotton.

Carno didn't have the talent to perform the skill to hide bodies, but Geraldine Finch did. It was her voice that directed her grandson then, and it was her guidance now.

Carno had killed Alicia Redfern and Tammy Jo Greer. Probably testing his budding magic on those who angered him and those he deemed disposable. It all came together now.

Prentice stood up.

His punch landed square in Prentice's face, knocking her to the ground. He lifted her off the floor and carried her over his shoulder. Pain flooded her body.

"This is the kind of power Gretchen rejected," Geraldine said, her tone heavy with disgust.

"Why kill your own granddaughter?" Prentice couldn't see, but she could smell and hear.

"She rejected the goddess's teachings. You should

be elated we got rid of her," Carno said. She could hear the joy in his voice.

A disturbing picture became clearer. Prentice could see it all happen. Carno's frustration with Gretchen's behavior, his whining to Geraldine, and their plan to do the forbidden ritual. It would make Gretchen obey, in theory. The more Gretchen resisted, the more unraveled he became. The bruising on Gretchen's feet, the beating, and Gretchen's fight back were all proof.

"No. You tried the ritual to purge her disobedience. You failed. There's a reason the Order forbids its practice!" Prentice said.

She hit the ground hard, and Carno snatched off her blindfold. Judging by their expressions, she'd hit the target.

"I wanted to cleanse her aura," Carno started.

"You hated the person she was becoming—an independent woman," Prentice said.

"Shut up!" Geraldine slapped Carno's back. She stepped outside of his shadow.

"You performed a brutal and unrelenting assault on a member of your own flock. What's worse, she probably would've come around with time," Prentice said, laughing. "And you two think she was out of the goddess's will."

Geraldine took out a pipe and blew.

The dirt plume knocked the breath out of Prentice. It was like a kick in the stomach. She struggled to breathe. It burned through her like wildfire. Exhausted and faint, on the brink of collapse, she struggled to stand.

Her vision crumbled down to mere shadows. Barely breathing and rage filled, Prentice fought to move her hands. She realized she was in real danger.

"How effective are blind hawks?" Geraldine asked with a grunt.

Transfixed, Prentice couldn't move. Blind. Injured. But her hands could just reach her talons. That binding spell waned. She moved to grab their handles, when suddenly, Carno came from behind and placed her in a choke hold.

An attack like this left a mental imprint. What Carno and Geraldine didn't know was Prentice had plenty experience being blind. She slammed her elbow into Carno's unprotected ribcage. He fell back, wheezing, and let go. He wasn't much of a fighter and barely twenty years old.

Prentice didn't give him a moment to breathe. She pulled her talons out of their holsters, pivoted around, and fired. She could hear his noisy attempts to get air. Using that, she tracked him and fired again. Carno grunted, but then she could feel more than see Geraldine moving toward her. The older woman was surprisingly fast on her feet. Her pipe was in her hand.

Prentice moved to avoid her.

Where had they taken her? She had to be on the

Finch property still. But they wouldn't take her somewhere where she'd be heard or seen by the girls or Bella. No, this little event was just for the three of them.

"What do you think you're going to do? Kill me? The Order will have so many hawks and condors flying over this place, you'll be begging for mercy." Prentice waited, talons out, listening.

"Missed me," Carno snarled and punched her right in the face.

He didn't retreat fast enough, and Prentice managed to slam the butt of her right talon into his face. He howled in pain. Honing in on his anguished cries, she fired again. This time her talon found its mark. He screeched.

"Carno!" Geraldine shouted. "That's it, you filthy bird."

With rapid speed, Prentice replaced her talons and ran. She couldn't see clearly, but as she moved, she took out her pen dagger. She pricked her finger and whispered, "*Cacher.*"

She felt the ground around her. Rough dirt. The scent of horses and manure hung heavy in the air. Could they be foolish enough to take her to the horse barn?

"Where'd she go?" Geraldine asked.

Carno groaned out an answer. "She shot me!"

"We have to find her," Geraldine said. Silence

and then, "Your little carnival magic won't save you, Hawk."

A *thrumming* sound blared just before the ground quaked beneath Prentice. It broke apart, and Prentice had to keep shifting to avoid falling into open fissures. One of the benefits of using the *Cacher* spell was her sight returned.

Blood magic repelled weaker earth magic. A rush of energy coursed through Prentice as her ancestors' blood magic surged. She felt like a dead person—sucking in oxygen but not alive.

The shadowy figures sharpened as her vision cleared. Once she could see, she managed to climb up a neighboring tree, using her wings to propel her upward. She could taste blood in her mouth, and she spat it out discreetly. She found the lowest branch and rested on it. Below her, Geraldine and Carno searched the area in front of the barn, along the sides, and in the rear. Carno's injury, in the upper shoulder, bled through his clothing. He moved sluggishly. They met back at the front of the barn.

"She's got to be around here somewhere." Geraldine's hands burned scarlet as the earth magic, pulling from the earth's core, forced the ground to break apart.

Unable to remain upright, Carno collapsed and lay crumpled in front of one of the stalls, bleeding where her talons had found their target.

Horses complained at the disturbance. They whinnied and pranced around.

"Grandmother…," Carno cried. He reached out for her. "It's bad. I'm bleeding."

"Curse you! You whining brat! Put some pressure on it." Geraldine whirled around on him. "Bob!"

Robert came out of a side door of the house. Not far from the front of the horse barn where they were located. As he headed toward them, Prentice had to decide what to do next. She couldn't contact anyone on her caller without them hearing. Her fading spell would keep her hidden for only so long.

Geraldine's hands cooled, and the ground fissures closed back up. No doubt, Geraldine had managed to hide those bodies and then, when she wanted, had the earth belch them back up.

Carno moaned and his body went limp.

Below her, Robert reached them. Geraldine pointed to Carno. "He had an accident with the horses. Get him to the house and help him."

None of Carno's injuries could have come from a horse, but Robert didn't question it. He bent down to aid his grandson.

Carno whimpered. Once he'd collected him, Geraldine turned around and searched the area. The woman never looked up. Most people didn't. Prentice watched them head back into the house.

Once the door slammed closed, Prentice leapt from the branches. She stretched out her wings and flew across the Finches' landscape and landed in front of the gate.

As her boots touched the ground, she looked around for James. Sure enough, he was brushing down the horse a few feet from the gate when she landed.

"Hawk Tasifa, you do not look well." He hurried over to her.

"I'm not," she said and stumbled toward the carriage.

James rushed to assist her. With his help, she fell back into the seat.

"Take me to the dove."

"Your face…"

"Hurry!" Prentice shouted.

The adrenaline had blunted the pain, but now it waned, and the anguish came roaring back. It felt horrible to be beaten.

But she knew Carno felt worse.

It gave her no pleasure at all.

CHAPTER FOURTEEN

As night fell, the carriage rushed past brush, trees, and across uneven ground. Prentice hovered between consciousness and passing out as she bounced around on the seat. The horse neighed and its feet flew.

After some time, the carriage rolled to a stop at the church, and James clambered down. He wrenched open the door. His large hands gently roused Prentice and helped her out of the carriage.

"I got your call. What happened? What's wrong?" Balthazar raced up to them.

Drained, Prentice leaned on James for the support to stand. Her life-force still battled the double dousing of earth magic, but despite being weakened, she wanted to get back up there.

As Balthazar took in her condition, he became ashen, his eyes wide with concern. "Prentice..."

"I was attacked by Carno and Geraldine. They used earth magic," Prentice explained, adjusting her belt around her waist.

"What?" Balthazar grabbed her shoulders and searched her face as if trying to detect if she was joking or not.

"They killed Gretchen, Dove, and they tried to kill me. Carno has killed two other birds…"

"Slow down. You reek of magic," Balthazar said, guiding her toward the church.

"Send the eagles. Now," Prentice coughed out. There was a tinge of exasperation in her voice, and she repeated herself. "They attacked me. They should be detained at once."

Balthazar blinked, and then ran for his office.

Prentice watched him run ahead. Her knees buckled, but James caught her before she hit the pavement. He carried her into the office, where Balthazar spoke to Eagle Jamison.

"Get up there. I'll explain later," Balthazar shouted. "They attacked Hawk Tasifa. Yes, Carno and Geraldine. Do not make me repeat myself."

"All right, Dove. Keep your cloak on." Eagle Jamison ended the transmission.

Balthazar turned to Prentice. James placed her in a chair. Prentice looked up at him.

"Thank you, James. Sweet milk, please."

James frowned at her, clearly confused.

Balthazar huffed. "Go tell Molly the hawk needs

sweet milk. She'll know what to give you."

James nodded and hurried from the room.

Balthazar sat in the opposite chair, hovering on the edge of the seat. "You've been busy."

"Yes."

"Tell me everything."

Prentice tried to stand up, but he pushed her gently back down.

"The eagles are on their way to the Finch home. No one is going anywhere, so relax. Take your time and tell me what your investigation has discovered and what happened this afternoon."

Prentice sighed and she did.

When she finished, Balthazar stood, his face solemn, his hands in fists.

"This is horrible. I can't believe it."

"I know, but they're responsible for the deaths of three people, maybe five. We haven't found Boris or Brian Greer, yet. They had no qualms about hurting me. I'm proof of that, but remember, I see the unseen."

At the creak of the door opening, Prentice jumped, one of her talons out in an instant and pointed at the entrance.

James held up one hand and offered the glass of sweet milk in the other.

"Sorry." Prentice put the talon away.

James came into the study and handed her the glass. She smelled it before drinking a long gulp.

"Let me make sure I understand. You discovered Carno had access to both women, the roosters, prior to their bodies being identified on the church green. You believe Geraldine and Carno Finch killed Gretchen attempting the ritual and buried her here as well."

"Yes."

"Geraldine used earth magic to hide the bodies on the green. They used the path between the Finch residence and the church to transport the bodies, and then for some reason you don't know, the bodies were coughed up," Balthazar said.

"Yes. I think Geraldine wanted Gretchen found, and when she removed the spell from her body, the others came up as well. It's possible she didn't even know about them. I suspect they were all Carno." Prentice drank another long gulp.

"Evidence?"

She winced as she rubbed the knot at the base of her neck. "Witness statements, Alicia Redfern's bones and teeth located in the ashes, and Tammy Jo's hair recovered from her skeleton. Gretchen's body and Carno's broken fingernail snared in her hair. Plus, they literally just attacked me and confessed to having killed her. They tried to kill me because I discovered their sins."

Balthazar sat stunned. Prentice watched the information sink in and the dove process it.

After several minutes, he rose. "I'm going to the

Finches' home." Balthazar, already dressed in his ceremonial cloak, put his hat on and nodded at James. "Fetch the carriage. Midnight may be too exhausted for the ride out, so let's get Lightning."

It took Prentice a few seconds to realize he referred to the horses.

Balthazar believed her, and a huge weight lifted from her shoulders. Still feeling antsy, she rubbed her legs.

Prentice stood up too. The milk and its sweetness had soothed and strengthened her. The earth magic's effects had waned. She'd been resting in the church study for the last hour.

She still hurt, and the knot throbbed, sending an ache along her body. She finished the drink in another long gulp. "Let's go."

"I don't think you're..." Balthazar started but then trailed off. His lips pressed into a line. "What's the point? You're stubborn and will just fly over there anyway."

"You know me so well," Prentice said. She adjusted her utility belt and the gun holster.

She and Balthazar walked out to the front in quiet. They waited several long minutes while James switched out the horse to pull the carriage. She didn't know if the eagles would sit on the Finches all evening or not. The next steps would determine if she needed help from the Order or if the local nest could handle it.

The horse's clops echoed in the empty twilight. The carriage arrived and Balthazar got the steps out and held the door while Prentice entered.

Once in the carriage, Balthazar said, "You need time to heal. You should've stayed behind. I can handle this."

"They meant to kill me today. I don't want them escaping or fleeing."

"Where would they go? The Finches have deep roots here. Geraldine has nowhere else, and if you hurt Carno with one of those talons, he's not going anywhere either," Balthazar said.

"I want this resolved. Letting it go another day would be too long. I don't want evidence to go missing. What if they decide to kill the rest of the Finch household? No, I need to get them captured," Prentice said. "The eagles can prep for earth magic. Yes?"

"I did warn Jamison to be prepared for it," Balthazar said with a solemn nod.

"You know, you could've trusted me with this sooner." Balthazar looked dejected.

"I wanted to be sure before I came to you." Prentice watched the landscape unfold.

Darkness had fallen, and a lot of the trees were dark, shadowy figures. She could smell the river as they drew closer to the Finch residential neighborhood.

"I understand that, but these are my nesters," Balthazar said.

"That's exactly why I waited to tell you."

Balthazar crossed his arms and stared out the window.

Although Prentice had discovered who killed Gretchen and the other two women, the victory was bittersweet. She could still hear Bella's anguished, blood-curling scream; Darlene's grief, crying at her desk over the loss of Alicia; and the idea someone would have to tell Tammy Jo's family that their wife and mother wasn't coming home.

Emotionally raw, Prentice closed her eyes and tried to meditate, to center herself before confronting the Finches. It was no good.

She looked across to Balthazar. He sat with his legs crossed, and his folded hands rested on his knee. A tranquility had settled over him, despite the approaching confrontation. Was he trying to reconcile the two people he knew versus the two she described?

"It's important to remember the person, not the tragedy," Prentice said.

He nodded, numbly. "Hoot."

"Hoot."

As THE CARRIAGE approached the Finch residence, Prentice made out two eagles standing at the mouth of the street with a wooden blockade. The street lanterns made little illuminated circles, but in front of the actual cul-de-sac, torches had been erected.

Eagle Jamison had taken their warning to be vigilant seriously. One of the eagles approached the carriage and peered inside.

"Hoot, Dove Balthazar," greeted the eagle. Prentice didn't recognize this one, a woman, with wide shoulders, shiny hair, and beautiful brown eyes.

"Hoot, Eagle Williamson. Let us through." Balthazar spoke in a calm, smooth tone, one lacking urgency despite the situation. Doves had that quality to soothe ruffled feathers. Prentice didn't know if it came from magic talent or a taught skill.

"Yes, Dove." Eagle Williamson stepped back from the carriage and waved to the eagles at the blockade.

Once beyond the blockade, James parked the carriage next to the Finches' front gate. To her surprise, it stood ajar, gaping open, and eagles walked in and out of it. Neighbors had emerged from their homes too and stood whispering about all the commotion. All the activity swirled around them. Ahead, she saw two covered carriages located in front of the Finches' home.

Prentice and Balthazar walked up to the eagle standing guard at the gate.

Eagle Smith greeted them.

"Hoot, Dove Balthazar and Hawk Tasifa," Eagle Smith said. He wore his usual uniform and stood with his hands on his hips. "Eagle Jamison is in the house. I have orders to take you to him."

Screaming broke through the murmurs of the spectators. Eagle Smith grimaced.

Balthazar frowned as he looked up to the house. "Is that Geraldine?"

Eagle Smith nodded. "Yes, Dove. She's been screaming at us since we arrived."

Prentice couldn't make out the words, but it became apparent that Geraldine Finch was unraveling.

"Give me a lantern and take us up." Prentice didn't like the anxious moments unfolding. She had a feeling in her feathers about the daunting task ahead.

Geraldine Finch had proven herself to be a dangerous and crafty individual. Carno's recklessness could be just as violent.

Eagle Smith handed a lantern over to her. He had another at his feet. An open carriage waited at the gate. Prentice and Balthazar climbed up into the carriage, and the eagle driver turned to greet them.

"Let's go." Prentice gestured toward the Finches' home.

They traveled up the long pathway that led to the door. Like the gate, it too stood open. Voices poured out of the opening. One of them sounded like Carno. His ramblings were explosive, but none of the eagles stationed at the front door paid any attention.

Prentice entered and headed down the long

hallway toward the rantings' origin. They found Eagle Jamison standing in front of the fireplace and three more eagles positioned in strategic places in the grand living room. They all bore guns and stony expressions. It looked like Balthazar's warning had been heeded, all disarray had been restrained, except Geraldine.

When she spied them coming into the room, she stopped talking.

"Hoot, Dove, Hawk Tasifa," Eagle Jamison said, his arms crossed over his wide chest.

"Hoot," Balthazar said in way of greeting.

Despite the confident looks and talk, Prentice could tell the doubts simmering under the surface. Nothing had been done to suppress Geraldine's power, and that stunned Prentice.

Once he reached Jamison, Balthazar turned to face the adult Finches, all seated on various couches. The three younger children must have been sent to other sections of the house. Prentice stood off to the side, by one of the windows, watching.

Carno hadn't died, but he had been patched up with bandages. Bruises decorated his face, and he didn't have on a shirt. He made faces at the eagles, taunting them from his position beside his grandmother on the central couch.

"What is she doing here?" Geraldine shouted. "Get out of my home!"

"Sit down," Eagle Jamison thundered.

"You're not going to tell me how to behave in my own home, Jamison." Geraldine lashed out at the eagles, at Balthazar, and at Prentice in a string of angry noise.

"Quiet!" Balthazar clapped his hands, and the boom reverberated throughout the house. It silenced everyone. It dawned on Prentice that Geraldine had decided to talk her way out of this.

James's words came back to mind. Of course she would. That had worked on everyone her entire life. Why would this time be any different?

Prentice shook her head. Geraldine's judgment was impaired.

Bella and Oliver sat across from Skylar and her husband.

"Dove, what is going on? Why are all these eagles in our house? Eagle Jamison won't tell us anything except to wait for you to arrive," a bewildered Skylar asked.

Balthazar swept toward the central couch to Bella and Oliver. Alarm came over Bella. Alert, she stood up. Visibly shaking, she let go of Oliver's hand.

"I can't catch my breath, but I know why you're here. Hawk Tasifa told me today. I…I can't believe it. He's my son."

Balthazar invoked his soothing timbre. "If the hawk already informed you, then you know she sees what is unseen. You also know, in your heart, Bel,

Carno hasn't fulfilled the family's expectations. He's perverted the goddess's guidelines and tenets."

Bella choked back tears. "No."

"He's a killer," Prentice interjected. "Every encounter he had with those who disagreed with him resulted in their deaths."

Balthazar hissed at her to be quiet. When he turned back to Bella, he guided her to sit back down. He turned to the adjacent seats where Carno had crawled back, attempting to disappear into the cushions.

"Now. Carno Finch is hereby charged with the slaying of Gretchen Finch…."

"No! By the goddess, no!" Bella cried.

Oliver held her tight, but he too was shattered. Shaking and crying, he didn't say a word.

Prentice waited to see Carno's explosive rage invoke his magic. Her hands inched down to her talons. A supercharged energy reverberated through the room. It shivered across her skin and her feathers.

Jamison nodded at one of the eagles, and she stalked over to Carno's place on the couch.

"Stand," the eagle commanded.

Whether from fear or defiance, Carno struggled to stand. The eagle snatched him by his non-injured arm and spun him around to confine his wrists. She tied his wrists together with a leather strap, making sure it was tight.

"No, Dove. This isn't right. You'll regret this. Hear me?" Geraldine said.

"...Alicia Redfern, and Tammy Jo Greer," Balthazar finished. He looked over to Bella and Oliver. "I'm sorry. Hawk Tasifa has conclusive evidence of his guilt."

Balthazar returned his attention to Carno.

"I did nothing! Nothing!" Carno shouted. "They made great fertilizer for the grounds!" He dissolved into tears. "Gretchen should've obeyed."

"Shut up! Shut up!" Bella shot off the couch, ran up to her son and slapped him.

Carno started crying out, "Grandmother! Help! Help me! Wait."

A second eagle raced up to Carno and fitted a white ball into his mouth.

Carno's eyes grew to the size of saucers at the sight of the gag. He and the female eagle struggled, but she won out due to sheer size and strength. She handed the gag's tie to the eagle behind Carno and he tied it tight.

Bella stood back; her hands covered her mouth. "Is this necessary?"

"It's to prevent casting," the female eagle said.

"He can't cast," Bella said, confusion forcing her to frown.

"He can," Prentice said. "My face is proof. The dead bodies of Alicia and Tammy Jo are also evidence Carno can cast earth magic."

"You really are a shallow human being, Carno," Skylar said, disgust wrinkling her face.

"You're a fragile woman," Geraldine said to her daughter.

Skylar stood up, glared at her mother, and stalked from the room. Her husband followed.

Bella whirled to her mother. "Earth magic? You taught him? You went against my wishes? You didn't have the right. He's *our* son, not yours."

"No right? I have *every* right. This is my family. As guardian, I will do everything in my power to protect it, and I did," Geraldine said. "None of you had the strength Carno does."

Carno's muffled shrieks grew faint as the eagles moved him down the hallway and out of the room.

"I have never known you to be so toxic," Bella said to her mother.

"I was following the goddess's divine plan," Geraldine said. "Gretchen was in great peril, Bel. You and Oliver failed her by letting her run off with that rooster and just ignore the teachings."

"You yearned for control of her. Just like you did with me and Skylar. Just like you do with everything! Well, I'm not you, and neither was Gretchen," Bella shot back.

"Even the goddess's work contained tales of persecution!" Geraldine declared.

"That's not on the goddess's path. Children follow their parents' direction, Geraldine. You subverted that bond and betrayed those to your daughters," Balthazar said, shaking his head in disappointment.

Geraldine turned her attention to him. "I betrayed no one."

"You slay your own granddaughter. That's a staunch and clear betrayal of trust," Eagle Jamison said.

The realization finally hit Bella and she groaned. "You *knew?*"

Balthazar said, "She did more than know, Bel."

"What?" Bella gave a nervous giggle.

"She killed herself! Refusing to follow the goddess's teachings, Gretchen would've died in the outer shell's slimy membrane. She was untamed. I tried to save her," Geraldine said to Balthazar.

"You and Carno subjected her to *The Obirt*, a ritual forbidden due to the fact people routinely died from it and it failed to bring about the desired obedience," Prentice explained.

Oliver glared. "You used *The Obirt* on our daughter?"

Bella joined him, plopping down in the seat beside him and putting her head in her hands.

Balthazar gaped. He looked from Prentice to Geraldine.

The Finch matriarch smoothed her hair back. "I've already explained it, Oliver. I won't repeat it because you can't keep up."

"Enough! Geraldine Finch, you are hereby charged with the slaying of Gretchen Finch, the attempted slaying of Hawk Prentice Tasifa, and the abuse of deceased persons," Balthazar said. His tone remained strong and clear.

Jamison nodded, and another eagle walked over to Geraldine Finch. He gestured for her to stand. She refused, crossing her arms and clucking her tongue.

Balthazar sighed and bent down to Geraldine. Prentice watched as he leaned in and spoke in soft whispers to her. The eagle stood beside the couch with the leather restraints in hand. He kept his eyes ahead, giving the dove and his nester privacy.

After a few hot murmurs and angry mumbling, Balthazar stood and said to the eagle, "She's ready."

Geraldine stood up, marched around the couch, and put her hands behind her back.

Prentice had a wretched feeling in her heart and an uneasy one in her feathers. The woman's calm demeanor didn't sit right.

"Get out of my house!" Geraldine thundered.

Prentice spied the scarlet spark before Balthazar spoke. In a blink, both talons fired.

Geraldine's magic managed to lift the flooring under Balthazar's feet, sending him crashing to the ground before both talons' bullets found their mark. Another section of the floor collided with some of the eagles, knocking them back into the corridor.

The Finch matriarch screamed and fell backward onto the eagle attempting to restrain her.

Shouts, screams, and crying melded into chaotic noise. More eagles spilled into the room. Prentice's ears rang, but she realized almost too late that Geraldine had blocked Balthazar's calming tongue and used a ruse of compliance. She scrambled over to Geraldine.

"Get the gag!" Jamison roared.

Hollering in pain, Geraldine rolled around the floor. The eagle managed to get her arms behind her in the ensuring chaos, but her constant moving and smearing of blood made her job more difficult.

Prentice snatched the gag from one of the eagles and pinched Geraldine's nose until she opened her mouth. Once she did, Prentice shoved the small white gag ball into her mouth and released her nose. She passed the flaps back and the eagle secured them. Unable to strike Prentice, Geraldine thrust her body to hurt her.

Balthazar crawled over to Geraldine on his knees.

"Don't worry, Dove. She'll live," Prentice said.

Geraldine ranted and cursed behind the gag. Balthazar leaned close to her and whispered until she went still and quiet. Unable to block him this time, the once powerful Finch woman became almost mute.

In the chaos of the arrest, Eagle Jamison had raced out, but now returned with a raven in tow. She wore a red headdress and a long, flowing dress. She crouched down beside Geraldine but spoke to all present.

"Who shot her?"

"Me." Prentice raised her hand.

"What kind of ammunition?"

"Silver-plated."

"I see." The raven doctor raised both eyebrows and dug around Geraldine's injuries, cutting through fabric as she did so. She moved swiftly, nimble fingers brushing across inflamed skin and torn muscle and tendons. "Move her to my clinic. I need to operate to pull these out. Get these restraints off."

"No, they stay on. She's a caster." Jamison shook his head.

"Fine, but once she gets to surgery, those have to come off," Dr. Little said.

"I can't take any more of this! Get the children. We're leaving." Bella fled the room in tears.

"Ollie, as your dove, I am here to counsel your family during this difficult time," Balthazar said. "Let me know when you return."

Oliver, his eyes fixed and glazed, nodded, before following Bella without another word to anyone. Eagle Jamison watched them go.

Two vultures arrived and hoisted Geraldine onto the stretcher. Throughout all of this, Geraldine didn't utter a word.

"Dove, what did you say to her?" Prentice asked.

Balthazar wiped his face and got to his feet. "I told her to be silent."

Eagle Jamison joined them. "We're taking Carno over to Bailey tonight. They've got secure holding for magic-users and mages. Williamson and Keyes will keep watch of Geraldine and bring her down once the doctor clears her."

"Okay. I'll head over there as well." Balthazar took in the blood on his robes and sleeves.

Jamison clapped him on the back. "It's been the kind of night you want to end but never seems to."

Prentice followed Jamison across the expansive room and down the wrecked hallway. She climbed over the crevice and made her way to the front door, still ajar. The remaining eagles had followed the guilty out.

Once outside and seated in the eagle carriage, she glanced back up at the beautiful home. Carno and Geraldine had crafted a false world of following the goddess's will and teachings. Tonight, that world had imploded, leaving nothing but carnage in its wake.

The truth is light. A goddess scripture in the peace tenet.

Hawks brought truth to light, by seeing what could not be seen by ordinary eyes. Instead of peace, Prentice's experience had found people hated hawks for this reason.

The results were dark, never light.

CHAPTER FIFTEEN

TWO DAYS LATER

Prentice placed her bags at the foot of the carriage. James hoisted them onto the back, securing each one with a broad, leather strap. Her train from Gould would depart in an hour, and it would take them about that long to get to Bailey's train depot. The rain conveyed the sadness she felt. Balthazar stood under a bright yellow umbrella. His mouth struggled not to pout and instead became a twisted mix of grin and disappointment.

"I heard from the dove in Bailey. Both Geraldine and Carno Finch are in custody. Geraldine appears to be recovering from her injuries. They're in separate birdcages, so I doubt either of them are happy," Balthazar said.

"And the rest of the family?" Prentice asked as she turned to face him fully.

"Vacationing in Adams Mountains. The Finches have a cabin there."

"Good for them."

Balthazar smiled. "Another tidbit that will brighten your day. Both Boris and Brian arrived home yesterday. They've been over in Heather working on the railroad for the last two weeks."

"They didn't tell their parents?" Prentice shook her head.

Balthazar shrugged. "Boris said they left word for their parents. Somehow the note got misplaced, tossed out or something. Whatever the case, they're safe and accounted for. You thought *we* were backward, the folks over in Heather Nest..."

"I didn't."

"Yes, you did. You don't have to be a hawk to see that, Prentice," Balthazar said and laughed.

"So, that's it," Prentice said.

"Indeed."

She bowed and then straightened. "The Order will submit a bill for my services. I gave my testimony to Eagle Jamison this morning, and the evidence has been delivered to his possession. This concludes my investigation, Dove."

Balthazar nodded. "I understand. Thank you."

"You're welcome. Contact the Order if you find you need my services again."

Prentice got into the carriage for what would be the last time. Droplets of rainwater cascaded down the windows and cast shadows throughout the interior. She missed her home and longed to put the horrid events of Gould and the Finches behind her. She longed for curry and smoked meats.

Three hard knocks made her jump seconds before the door wrenched open.

Balthazar stuck his head inside. "Sorry! The carrier pigeon dropped this off about an hour ago. It has your name on it."

He held out the crumpled, damp envelope to her. His gaze hovered on her.

"Goodbye," he whispered and zipped out of the carriage, slamming the door closed as he left.

Prentice used her pen dagger to slice open the sealed letter. The Order's winged purple wax seal spoke to its official authenticity. Inside, she groaned. It didn't look like she would get to go home after all.

Hawk Tasifa—
Your services have been requested in the Sulidae Egg.
Arrive within two days and greet Dove Raz Haq.
The situation as we know at this time:
Missing sacred goddess's feathered crown.
Proposed magical use.
Possible suspects: Rook Bjorn Renner
The truth is light. Bring it forth as hawks see what is unseen.
Peace,

Cardinal Wick

Prentice pinched the bridge of her nose. The carriage had already jerked her forward. Sulidae Egg caused a knot to form in her belly. Rook Renner stood as one of the oldest, most respected rooks, but now he stood accused of theft.

It didn't make any sense, but Prentice would get down there to see what others couldn't.

She banged on the carriage ceiling. "James, kick it into high gear. I've got another investigation to get to!"

James replied, "Yes, hawk."

The End

Love it? Hate it? REVIEW it for us while it's fresh on your mind.

BONUS

First look at the next Kingdom of Aves Mystery, *A Theft Most Fowl*

The University of Sulidae was the oldest one in Aves. Originally, its location resided in the Auduban Nest, close to Lanham Egg, home of the Order. Political infighting forced the intellectual thinkers to put some distance between themselves and the Order. Experience taught them that the closer you got to power, the harder it was to survive. In response, the Order opened an intelligence file on university members. Despite its history of hurt feelings and tensions on both sides, many of those within the Order's rank traveled and studied at the university's new location in Sulidae Egg, in Edmonds Nest. It sat on the banks of the Plume River at the apex of the Audubon and

Edmonds nests. The egg revolved around the university. The campus was its own island in the egg.

Rook Bjorn Renner's entire life orbited around the university, most importantly the Sulidae Museum of the Goddess. As curator, Rook Renner's true passion and what he spent his life doing, was collecting goddess artifacts. As a renowned expert in all things goddess, Renner received a constant stream of requests to verify and validate recently discovered treasures. Over time, his teachings gained more urgency around authenticity.

Prentice found it strange that a devoted bird like Rook Renner would steal the Five-Feathered Crown. Why now? Why only that one? Why not something less copious?

It didn't add up.

Someone broke into the museum and stole the Five-Feathered Crown. In the ensuing massive manhunt, the eagles, the security for all eggs, searched, but came up empty. Request for assistance from the public produced nothing, according to the reports. No doubt, Rook Renner was frantic with worry.

She sipped her tea as ideas formulated in her mind. Drinking Earl Gray became a simple pleasure among the stickiness of investigative work.

The ancient cogwheel train raced across the way, and it gently rocked as it chugged its way through the Edmonds Nest. She'd left the Bailey's rolling hills and the Adams Mountains, their snow-capped tips. They grew smaller in the distance along with the red roofs of Bailey Egg. Now, two days later, she meandered Adams River. She missed Gould, and if the circumstances changed, she'd return again, but not for work. She'd been on the train for two days and Sulidae appeared in sight. Thankfully, she had the sleeping car to herself. The night seat folded down for a bed. Features included carved wood paneling, pressed metal ceiling, frost glass, and lamp oils and other ornate decorations. She sat in the small overstuffed chair and removed her notepad.

When not on an active investigation, Prentice wore casual clothing. Her dark wings identified her as a hawk. Her sapphire headdress bore silver embroidered wings, and it matched her frock. A silver satin scarf draped from her neck and across her left shoulder. She put away the boots in exchange for flat, closed-toe sandals. Sulidae lay in the Edmonds Nest, just southwest of Lanham. The weather remained warm throughout the year due to the Avian Sea currents. She dressed accordingly, but only by chance. Unable to return home from her last case for a change of clothes, Prentice happened to have cooler clothing packed. No doubt, the rook sowed the seeds of his own demise with his erratic behavior.

The train bumped over the railroad tracks as it slowed into Lizard Mountain Train Station, the sun set. The whistle announced their arrival, and Prentice disembarked with her luggage and satchel. She already missed the cool mountains of Gould. Along the platform, coachmen carried signs advertising their services. She secured one, and in no time, she found herself seated in a carriage, her luggage bags secured outside, in the rear, and her driver seated in front. Two beautiful horses pulled them away from the train station and into the night.

Even early supper time, the egg bustled with life. Students clutched heavy satchels and walked or bicycled through the streets. People clustered together in casual conversations at outdoor cafes, illuminated by votive candles. The pedestrians hiked alongside cyclists with ease in a practiced rhythm.

In the hushed carriage interior, Prentice embraced the nostalgia rushing over her. She hadn't been here in years, not since graduation. Outside the carriage window, the Plume River glistened as it snaked its way through the egg. A clear sky put the constellations on display, and she warmed at the memory of nights spent in Rook Ioan's astronomy class, charting and memorizing the heavens, gazing through telescopes and listening to how they came to be. A hawk was never lost as long as they had the sky.

"We're here." The coachman wrenched open the door and disappeared around to the carriage's rear. He clambered up the short ladder and threw down her luggage bags. They smacked the ground.

"By the goddess, be careful!" Prentice bellowed as she exited. *Vultures!*

The coachman came back around with said baggage stuffed under both arms. He glared at her as he placed them beside her. The tight, grayish skin bore thin scars. The bright scarlet birthmark across his sharp nose drew attention away from his beady dark eyes.

"Thank you." Prentice took five birdsongs from her leather pouch. She dropped the copper coin with the 5 emblazed on the tail and the goddess's likeness on the front into the coachman's gloved hand.

"Evening." The man bowed, his face softened by the tip, before leaping up to the driver's seat. His agility surprised her. His girth didn't hinder his movements at all.

She turned her attention to the pristine cathedral that consumed the center entrance of the university campus. The air was heavy with the thick fragrance of frankincense and sage. A cobblestoned maze of dark corridors threaded through the grounds and connected the buildings. Dark hallways stretched out in a monolithic maze of nooks and crannies. The illusion of safety had been shattered, and tension hung in the air. It was impossible to take in at a glance the enormity of the university.

Ahead, a figure appeared in the growing dark. Lit lanterns illuminated the square. She could make out the red turban atop a head. A sudden strong wind billowed his dark robes. Prentice didn't need her hawk abilities to recognize Rook Renner. Her jaw tightened as he approached.

Once the wizened old man reached her, he wasted no time embracing her.

"Hoot, Prentice." Renner pulled her close.

His voice was stronger than Prentice expected.

She returned his hug but pulled back. "Hoot, Rook, but how are you here? Shouldn't you be in a cell?"

Rook Renner's jovial face held bemusement. He didn't seem distraught. "It would seem my rapidly eroding reputation has kept that action at bay."

His raw-bone features decorated with broad red lines beneath each eye and a vertical one from his forehead down to his chin disappeared beneath a bushy white beard.

"Come. I'm glad you're here." He clasped her hand in his bony one. The soft flesh palm spoke to the rook never doing physical labor in his life.

"Where?" she asked.

He motioned ahead. "I've had a small instructor apartment set up for you."

Prentice took back her hand. "An apartment? Rook, you know I'm hear to investigate you and the theft…"

She trailed off. She had a sinking feeling about this.

Rook Renner raised his hand. The silver rings he wore caught the pale moonlight.

"I'm aware. It's a studio, nothing luxurious. The Order cannot say I attempted to bribe you. My status may not be what it once was at court, but I'm greatly injured at this intrusion. The sooner we get this resolved, the sooner I can get back to my work.

"Rook…" Prentice felt sorry she hinted at it.

But she didn't travel here to rekindle their student-instructor relationship. She'd been assigned to this case, and she had a job to do.

See the unseen.

She adjusted her satchel across her torso and then hoisted her luggage.

"Lead the way."

Rook Renner, with a gracious smile, said, "Follow me."

End Excerpt

Pre-Order *A Theft Most Fowl: A Kingdom of Aves Mystery*

ABOUT NICOLE GIVENS KURTZ

Nicole Givens Kurtz's short stories have appeared in over 40 anthologies of science fiction, fantasy, and horror. Her novels have been finalists for the EPPIEs, Dream Realm, and Fresh Voices in science fiction awards. Her work has appeared in the Bram Stoker® Finalist, *Sycorax's Daughters,* Baen's *Straight Outta Tombstone* and Onyx Path's *The Endless Ages Anthology*.

Visit Nicole's other worlds online at Other Worlds Pulp, www.nicolegivenskurtz.net.

Nicole's Whereabouts on the Web:

Other Worlds Pulp-http://www.nicolegivenskurtz.net
Join Nicole Givens Kurtz's Newsletter-http://www.nicolegivenskurtz.net/newsletter
Follow Nicole on Twitter-@nicolegkurtz
Follow on Facebook-http://www.facebook.com/nicolegkurtz